FIRST DEGREE MURDER

LANTERN BEACH PD, BOOK 3

CHRISTY BARRITT

COMPLETE BOOK LIST

Squeaky Clean Mysteries:

#1 Hazardous Duty

#2 Suspicious Minds

#2.5 It Came Upon a Midnight Crime (novella)

#3 Organized Grime

#4 Dirty Deeds

#5 The Scum of All Fears

#6 To Love, Honor and Perish

#7 Mucky Streak

#8 Foul Play

#9 Broom & Gloom

#10 Dust and Obey

#11 Thrill Squeaker

#11.5 Swept Away (novella)

#12 Cunning Attractions

#13 Cold Case: Clean Getaway

#14 Cold Case: Clean Sweep

While You Were Sweeping, A Riley Thomas Spinoff

The Sierra Files:
#1 Pounced
#2 Hunted
#3 Pranced
#4 Rattled
#5 Caged (coming soon)

The Gabby St. Claire Diaries (a Tween Mystery series):
The Curtain Call Caper
The Disappearing Dog Dilemma
The Bungled Bike Burglaries

The Worst Detective Ever
#1 Ready to Fumble
#2 Reign of Error
#3 Safety in Blunders
#4 Join the Flub
#5 Blooper Freak
#6 Flaw Abiding Citizen
#7 Gaffe Out Loud
#8 Joke and Dagger (coming soon)

Raven Remington
Relentless 1
Relentless 2 (coming soon)

Holly Anna Paladin Mysteries:

    #1 Random Acts of Murder

    #2 Random Acts of Deceit

    #2.5 Random Acts of Scrooge

    #3 Random Acts of Malice

    #4 Random Acts of Greed

    #5 Random Acts of Fraud

    #6 Random Acts of Outrage

    #7 Random Acts of Iniquity (coming soon)

Lantern Beach Mysteries

    #1 Hidden Currents

    #2 Flood Watch

    #3 Storm Surge

    #4 Dangerous Waters

    #5 Perilous Riptide

    #6 Deadly Undertow

Lantern Beach Romantic Suspense

    Tides of Deception

    Shadow of Intrigue

    Storm of Doubt

Lantern Beach P.D.

    On the Lookout

    Attempt to Locate

    First Degree Murder

    Dead on Arrive (coming in April)

Carolina Moon Series

Home Before Dark

Gone By Dark

Wait Until Dark

Light the Dark

Taken By Dark

Suburban Sleuth Mysteries:

Death of the Couch Potato's Wife

Fog Lake Suspense:

Edge of Peril

Margin of Error (coming soon)

Cape Thomas Series:

Dubiosity

Disillusioned

Distorted

Standalone Romantic Mystery:

The Good Girl

Suspense:

Imperfect

The Wrecking

Standalone Romantic-Suspense:

Keeping Guard

The Last Target

Race Against Time

Ricochet

Key Witness

Lifeline

High-Stakes Holiday Reunion

Desperate Measures

Hidden Agenda

Mountain Hideaway

Dark Harbor

Shadow of Suspicion

The Baby Assignment

The Cradle Conspiracy (coming soon)

Nonfiction:

Characters in the Kitchen

Changed: True Stories of Finding God through Christian Music (out of print)

The Novel in Me: The Beginner's Guide to Writing and Publishing a Novel (out of print)

CHAPTER ONE

MORIAH ROBERTS SAT up in bed, her gaze skittering across the room. As the cheerful yellow walls came into view, her shoulders relaxed. There was no need to be alarmed. She was safe here.

She closed her eyes and ran her hands across the soft sheets of her warm, clean bed.

Safe. Secure. Sheltered.

Moriah loved the sound of those words.

As of four days ago, this room was her home.

No longer did she have to stay in the rundown RV with the drafty windows, where she'd been housed since she'd first arrived at Gilead's Cove more than a month ago. Those sleeping quarters had been cold. So cold. Frigid enough that it sometimes made Moriah miss her West Virginia home.

But not anymore.

As Moriah leaned back on her palms, an ache tore

through the skin near her shoulder. The burn wound there was better now, thanks to some ointment that had been given to her, but when her skin pulled, the mark screamed with discomfort.

"You've been refined by the fire." Moriah closed her eyes and recited Gilead's words. "Refined by the fire, and afterward you'll come forth as gold."

Her suffering was actually intended to make Moriah stronger. She hadn't been able to see that at first, but in the past two days, the wisdom had become clear. The trials in her life would give her thick skin.

"You're going to be gold, Moriah," she whispered, squeezing the sheets between her fingers. "Pure gold. You'll live as a chosen one, set apart, and given purpose."

Moriah stood and glanced around. She was now staying in a tiny bedroom located above the community center—also known as the Meeting Place—here at the Cove. The best part about staying here was that Gilead, her fiancé, had a room across the hall.

In three days, they would be married. The two would become one, joined together under God. And what God joined together, no man should tear apart.

No one.

A smile stretched across her face. Moriah was finally living the life she'd always dreamed about.

She walked to her dresser and began to apply some lotion that Gilead had given her. The cream smelled so lovely, like roses, and Moriah secretly delighted in the fact that she was the only person here at the Cove allowed such frivolous items. Gilead had even given her a stuffed teddy bear the other day—further evidence of how much he loved her.

Gilead said the process of transforming Moriah into his bride was like Esther being prepared to be chosen by King Xerxes. Moriah had begun a series of beauty regimens. She'd been given facials. Hair treatments. Steam baths.

All so she could be pristine and lovely on her wedding day.

Moriah smiled again and continued to rub the lotion on her face, neck, and chest.

As a knock sounded, Moriah padded across the wood floor that had been painted a dark red color. She cracked the door open and saw Ruth standing on the other side, her lips puckered in disdain.

"We need you downstairs." Ruth's words sounded crisp and left no room for argument. "Now."

The woman was her mentor, a mother figure, and her uninvited conscience, all rolled into one. Though Moriah appreciated having someone to watch over her, Ruth drove her up the wall with her reprimanding looks and self-righteous attitude. After Moriah married Gilead, getting rid of Ruth would be her first order of business.

"Is everything okay?" Moriah formed her words carefully, practicing speaking without her mountain accent.

Ruth's expression soured even more as her eyelids drooped and her lips pulled down in a frown. "We have someone new coming today, and Gilead would like for you to meet her."

Moriah's pulse quickened. "Someone new?"

The Cause was growing, receiving several new people each week. What was so special about this new person? Moriah had never been asked to "meet" anyone before.

"That's right. Dietrich is bringing someone in. Gilead thinks you're ready to be a mentor." Ruth sounded unconvinced and skeptical as her acerbic expression soured even more.

Moriah ignored her. "That's great. Let me get dressed, and I'll be right out."

Taking her time, Moriah pulled on her tunic, khakis, and sandals and went through her morning routine. As she met Ruth in the hallway several minutes later, her gaze traveled through the open office door across from her.

Gilead's office.

He was usually careful to keep the door closed. The man was private, and he valued his alone time, his space. Every great leader probably did.

An image on his computer caused Moriah to suck in a deep breath. Normally, she couldn't see the screen, but today the monitor had been turned to face the chairs on the other side of the desk, almost as if Gilead had been showing someone something.

The photo was of that police chief from here in Lantern Beach . . . the woman who'd tried to convince Moriah to leave Gilead's Cove. The one who'd painted Moriah's fiancé in a negative light. Who'd told her lies about what went on here.

Why in the world would her photo be on Gilead's computer screen?

Ruth followed her gaze, and she let out a soft *tsk*. "Why do you look worried, Moriah?"

Moriah snapped her attention back to the present, realizing her face had revealed too many of her thoughts. She needed to work on that if she was going to help lead this community with Gilead.

"Who said I was worried?" Moriah carefully kept a shield over her gaze this time.

Ruth stared at the computer and shrugged, her voice stone-cold as she said, "I'd be worried too."

Ruth's words froze Moriah's thoughts, froze her feet even, right where they were. "What do you mean?"

Ruth nodded toward the photo on the computer screen. "We value speaking honestly here."

"Of course. I want honesty."

Still, Ruth hesitated a moment. "Speaking as your mentor, I have to say . . . I've seen the way Gilead looks at that woman, the police chief. There's more there than a professional curiosity."

Moriah's heart pounded furiously. Certainly Ruth wasn't saying what Moriah thought she was. She had to be misunderstanding all of this. What Ruth said didn't fit the big picture. It didn't fit what Moriah knew about Gilead.

"What are you implying, Ruth?" Moriah refused to take another step until she figured this out. No way could she simply brush off this conversation and move on.

Ruth's eyebrows quirked upward, but her plain face still expressed her warning. "I'm not trying to rain on your parade, Moriah. I'm not. I'm just being realistic here. Men like Gilead can have it all. And they want it all. My ex-husband was the same way."

"You were married?" Why hadn't Moriah ever heard this about Ruth before? The woman seemed so miserable that Moriah couldn't imagine Ruth ever opening her heart to someone.

"For ten years."

Ten years? Ruth couldn't be any older than thirty . . . how old had she been when she got married?

It didn't matter. Ruth was using her own experiences to taint Moriah's perspective. Her mom had told her there would always be people who tried to ruin the good things in her life. That was exactly what Ruth was doing now.

"I understand that you may have had a bad marriage, but Gilead is different," Moriah said.

"You're right." Ruth smiled with only her eyes. "He's ordained. God speaks to him."

Moriah tugged at her shirt, trying to fight the

anxiety that nibbled away at her resolve. "God told Gilead to marry me."

Ruth let out a condescending laugh and lowered her voice. "Child, you know there's room in a marriage for more than one wife, don't you? Look at the Old Testament accounts."

The blood drained from Moriah's face. She hated it when Ruth called her child. But she hated what Ruth had said even more.

The woman wasn't right. She couldn't be right. Moriah refused to believe it.

"Gilead loves me. He chose me. God told him I was the one for him." Moriah's voice quivered as she said the words, and she silently reprimanded herself.

Ruth patted her back, still patronizing her. "And that's true. But that doesn't mean that God didn't tell him to marry someone else as well."

Moriah shook her head, unable to believe what she was hearing. Ruth didn't know what she was talking about. She was jealous.

That was it.

Ruth was just jealous because Gilead had chosen Moriah over Ruth.

Besides, there were other reasons why what Ruth had said couldn't be true.

"That police chief—Cassidy or whatever her name is," Moriah started. "She doesn't follow the Cause."

"I don't know what to tell you." Ruth shrugged

dismissively and took another step toward the stairway, signaling an end to the conversation. "I only know that Gilead looks at her like a man in the desert looks at water."

Nausea turned into Moriah's stomach. "The police chief is married."

"What God has ordained let no man stand in the way of."

Moriah's lips parted in shock. "You think God would tell Gilead to break up a marriage? Doesn't the Bible speak out against that?"

"The Lord works in mysterious ways."

"But He doesn't contradict Himself, right?" Moriah wasn't a biblical scholar, but she did remember a few things from Sunday school as a child.

Ruth let out a long sigh and stepped back toward Moriah, as if this conversation had exhausted her. "The old ways are gone, Moriah. Haven't you been listening to the words from Makir? You haven't been dreaming about your marriage while Gilead teaches us from the Good Book, have you?"

Makir was a lost book of the Bible that Gilead had discovered in the Middle East. He often liked to teach from it. He was God's chosen one.

And, on occasion, Moriah had drifted off into another world while Gilead spoke. She didn't mean to. But she had so much to look forward to. How could she not?

"You just need to let it be, Moriah." Ruth waved her

hand in the air flippantly. "There's no changing what's ordained to be. And Gilead has chosen you. Be happy."

Happy? Moriah couldn't be happy. Not after this conversation with Ruth.

A surge of anger rose up inside Moriah. Gilead was hers. No one else's.

She wouldn't share. She'd refuse.

As Cassidy Chambers' picture burned into her mind, so did Moriah's resolve. Nothing would get in the way of her happiness with Gilead. Nothing, and no one.

And Moriah would do whatever it took to ensure that.

CHAPTER TWO

"THANKS FOR MEETING ME HERE, CHIEF." Officer Billy Leggott stood by the woods that surrounded the property adjacent to the Lantern Beach lighthouse, a nervous flutter to his gaze.

"I'm still not sure why I'm here." Cassidy Chambers had gotten the call from the station as she drank her morning coffee.

Early mornings were her favorite part of the day—a time where she and her husband, Ty, chatted about the future, when they enjoyed the sunrise together or took a jog on the beach or shared breakfast before the craziness of everyday life set in.

But today that time had been interrupted by an ambiguous phone call.

Leggott had offered no details. He'd just told Cassidy that she needed to meet him here right away.

"Wayne Waters was out here fishing this morning,"

Leggott started, turning his back to the rising sun in the distance. "He's the one who made the discovery and phoned the station. Of course, I was the one on call. You'll want to see for yourself what he found. Follow me."

Leggott nodded toward the woods—a mix of live oaks and other short, shrubby trees, which formed a dense barrier for the island against the raging waters that pounded the shores. Pushing away her pre-coffee drowsiness, Cassidy followed after him, hoping this interruption was worth it.

Certainly, Leggott wouldn't have called her if this wasn't important. At this point in their professional relationship, he should know better.

When Cassidy had first met the man, he'd seemed incompetent. But she'd realized during her tenure as police chief that Leggott simply hadn't been properly trained. With a little nurturing, the man was shaping up to be a great officer, someone she was proud to be associated with.

Her department was finally coming together, and Cassidy didn't care what anyone said—she was honored to be their leader and hoped she wouldn't let them down.

Cassidy's curiosity grew as she stepped farther into the dense foliage. The light around her dimmed as tree branches formed a canopy of skeletal arms overhead. The deeper down the path she walked, the more the vegetation squeezed tighter. It brushed her legs and swept down lower and lower until Cassidy had to duck to avoid the leaves and vines.

As she ducked under another branch, her phone buzzed. She pulled it from her pocket and glanced at the screen. What now? Island life was supposed to be simple and full of slow mornings . . . mornings that started with two cups of coffee.

She'd been wrong. Things on Lantern Beach were *never* simple.

Cassidy read the text there, and the blood drained from her face.

I know who you are.

She blinked, unconvinced she was correctly understanding the meaning of the words. Her gaze traveled to a picture that loaded beneath the message.

It was an image of Cassidy. Only, it was the old Cassidy. The one who was a brunette. Who went by the name Cady Matthews. Who'd lived in Seattle. The detective who'd infiltrated a dangerous gang.

Cady Matthews was supposed to be dead.

But someone knew she wasn't.

Cassidy's heart thumped in her ears at the realization.

She glanced at the number. The area code was local.

Her heart thumped even harder. The noise drowned everything else until her pulse was all she could hear. Pounding. Pounding.

As she took another step, her gaze skittered around

her. Was the person who'd sent this message watching her now?

The forest and all its mysterious shadows stared back at her, taunting her.

"Everything okay?" Leggott asked, peering at her phone.

Quickly, Cassidy turned off the screen and shoved the device back in her pocket. No one else could know about her real identity. Only Ty and their friend Mac knew the truth—and sometimes Cassidy wondered if they were two too many people. Anyone who knew her real identity was in danger.

"Yeah, everything's fine." But Cassidy's thoughts still raced. How had someone gotten her number? How had they discovered she was here?

"So, anyway, you know we had that high tide here a few days ago, right?" Leggott's voice pulled her from the deep pit her questions tried to bury her in.

Cassidy stepped over some tree roots that snaked and knotted across the sandy ground. She needed to focus right now on whatever Leggott had called her here for. She'd have time to think about that text later.

She swallowed the fear that swelled in her gut and made sure her voice was steady as she said, "Yes, I remember the tide."

A particularly strong weather front had come in from the east, bringing rain with it, as well as pushing the water levels higher than usual. The roads had flooded, and the water had caused some minor damage to several houses near the shore.

"The storm created quite a bit of erosion," Leggott continued before taking a puff of his inhaler. The fluctuating weather here on the island had made his asthma go crazy lately. He'd even called in sick one day.

As a twig snapped in the distance, everything went eerily quiet around them.

Cassidy paused and glanced around.

Nothing but trees surrounded by hollows of tidal water stared back.

Something out here felt alive, though. More than alive. Something out here seemed to watch them.

It was probably nothing, Cassidy told herself. Maybe a fox or a deer. But she would remain on guard.

Especially after that text.

Dread continued to build up in Cassidy's chest as they walked down the path. Finally, they cleared the woods, and a sandy shoreline greeted them, along with a steady wind that cut across the island, dropping the temperature probably about ten degrees.

Cassidy pulled her coat closer, nodded at Wayne Waters, who stood near the edge of the path, and then turned back toward Leggott. "So . . ."

He pointed toward the woods several yards from the path they'd taken here. "Have a look."

Cassidy tromped across the sand and paused at the edge of the trees. She sucked in a breath at what she saw there.

It was . . . a skull.

Her gaze traveled the surrounding area. A ribcage and other bones poked from the nearby sand and underbrush.

It was a skeleton.

A human skeleton.

Unmistakably.

At one time, the bones had probably been buried here under a couple feet of earth. But the storm must have pulled the sand away, revealing this sad, shallow grave.

"There's more." Leggott's voice sounded grim.

Cassidy turned toward him, uncertain if she'd heard correctly. "More?"

He nodded beyond the first skeleton. Cassidy followed his gaze and saw another skull a few feet away.

"How many?" Cassidy's throat tightened as the question left her lips.

Leggott frowned. "I counted three."

Cassidy closed her eyes. They had a mass grave on their hands . . . and these bones didn't appear to be from settlers or Native Americans from decades past. No, these bones looked fresh.

She hated to do it, but Cassidy knew this was bigger than her small department could handle. She was going to have to call in backup . . . again.

CHAPTER THREE

TY CHAMBERS GRIPPED the pull-up bar he'd mounted to the underside of his house and felt his muscles burn as he lifted his body from the ground. Though the day was chilly, sweat rippled across his skin with each rep.

He would have preferred a morning jog on the beach with his wife to burn off some stress. But Cassidy had been called away to do her duty as police chief here on Lantern Beach.

Ty wondered what had happened on the island this time. The area just couldn't seem to catch a break lately with one crime after another bruising the otherwise peaceful community.

He supposed it was good for Cassidy's job security, but he'd hoped for a small reprieve from the craziness that had filled their schedules lately.

As he looked across his property, he spotted a

familiar figure strolling across the sandy lawn toward him.

Braden Dillinger.

Ty's friend was currently staying in one of the cabanas Ty had built at the back of his property, and Ty had asked to meet with him this morning. Braden was helping him with Hope House in exchange for a place to live.

The main house had been his grandfather's old beach cottage, a summer home Ty couldn't get enough of as a child. The property had been left to him when his grandfather passed away, which happened to be at the same time Ty had given up his job as a Navy SEAL.

He'd felt a new calling on his life—a call to start an organization to help those who'd been in the military but now faced major life changes and challenges, whether physical, emotional, or mental.

Ty's first one-week session had gone exactly as he'd planned. There'd been times of sharing, one-on-one times with a counselor, water sports, fishing, and community building.

It had been perfect.

But now, finances and some unexpected setbacks threatened to cancel the next session—unless Ty could think of a way to get things back on track. He didn't have much time to figure it out. His next group was scheduled to arrive in less than two weeks.

"Good morning!" Braden stopped a couple feet away.

Ty lowered himself from the bar, grabbed his workout towel, and wiped his face. "Morning."

"I'm jealous. You're getting in a workout already. I've got to step up my game."

"Yeah, well, you've had some other things on your mind. Things like planning a wedding." Ty grabbed his water bottle and took a sip. "Thanks for meeting with me. Why don't we head upstairs?"

Braden held up something in his hands. "Lisa insisted I bring some muffins. I think they're chocolate and zucchini, but Lisa insists they're delicious."

"Well, she's never let us down before."

As the two of them started up the steps, Ty turned toward his friend. "You ready for the big day?"

Braden was marrying local sweetheart and cooking genius Lisa Garth in a few days, and the whole island buzzed with excitement over it.

"I'm more than ready." Braden grinned from ear to ear. "I feel like the luckiest guy in the whole world."

Ty grinned. "I remember the feeling. Marrying Cassidy was the best decision I've ever made."

They stepped inside the house, and Braden slammed the door behind him. As he did, something clattered across the floor—something bigger than a nail but small enough that neither Ty nor Braden immediately spotted it.

Ty finally located the mystery object and plucked it from the floor. His gaze met Braden's, and he frowned.

"Someone planted a camera in the house," he muttered, realization washing over him.

"Why would someone do that?"

Ty pressed his lips together. There was more than one possibility.

And each of them left him with knots in his stomach.

———

THREE HOURS LATER, the wind still blew steadily as Cassidy and her team secured the area and continued to examine it for more clues as to what had happened here. Wayne Waters had been questioned, directed to remain quiet, and sent home. Her other officer, Dane Bradshaw, had also been brought in to help. All of that was until a team of investigators from the North Carolina State Bureau of Investigation arrived.

In the meantime, Lantern Beach's local medical examiner and physician, Doc Clemson, was on the scene, processing what he could.

Everyone would be here for a while—probably well into the night, if Cassidy had to guess.

Each of the graves had to be well documented. The soil had to be sifted through. The remnants of these human lives had to be carefully preserved and then moved for better examination and more testing.

The land where these bodies were found was a part of a National Seashore. With the easy water access, anyone could have dumped the bodies here. The only people who would come this far through the woods and on foot was the occasional fisherman, coming when the tide was just right to cast a line.

One thing was for sure: these bodies hadn't gotten here by themselves. Someone had left them. The question was: had these people been murdered, or was there another reason they'd been dumped in this location?

Whatever the intention, it was a crime to dispose of human remains in this manner. And the fact that three bodies were found together indicated that their deaths hadn't been accidental.

Cassidy hoped Clemson might be able to give them some more direction. This new discovery had almost—almost—taken her mind off that earlier text. Maybe the distraction would be good for her.

She knelt beside the doctor as he leaned over one of the skeletons. His glasses were perched at the end of his chubby nose, and his thin reddish-orange hair blew with the wind, revealing bald spots beneath. In his sixties and about twenty pounds overweight, being on the ground wasn't as easy as it had once been. Despite that, Clemson had a pad and pencil in hand, and nothing would stop him from doing his job.

"What do you think?" Cassidy couldn't get the image of the skull out of her mind. It hadn't been completely clean. No, remainders of life still clung to it like a last-ditch cry for help.

Clemson let out a grunt and stared at the skeleton in

front of him. "My initial assessment? Based on the decomposition and the elements, I'd guess these bodies have been here for four or five months. At least, these two have. The third one maybe for a little less."

That was what Cassidy had suspected—these weren't old bones from decades past. "Is there anything else you can tell about them?"

"Someone with the state will be able to tell you more. But we have two women and one man here. Two of them had straight teeth—meaning, they probably had some money and means growing up."

"Teeth are usually a good indication of a person's socioeconomic background," Cassidy said.

Clemson nodded and pushed his glasses up higher on his nose. "Exactly. But the third . . . her teeth have definitely never seen braces—or maybe not even a dentist, for that matter."

"Interesting."

Clemson stood, brushing the sand from his jeans. "Also, there's some hair left on the victims. Hair and fingernails, because they're made of keratin, decompose much more slowly than soft tissue. That said, one of the women had long gray hair, and the other two victims did not."

"So you're saying they're probably different ages?"

Clemson nodded. "Exactly.

"So, two women. One man. Different ages. Different socioeconomic backgrounds." Cassidy shook her head. "Victims usually fit a pattern."

"You're correct."

Cassidy would speculate more later. Right now, she needed all the information she could get until the North Carolina State Bureau of Investigation arrived. "What about manner of death? Any clues?"

"We really have four options here. Accident, suicide, natural causes, or murder." Clemson let out a long breath and frowned at the skeleton below him. "That said, I didn't see any broken bones or skull fractures. There's nothing to indicate there was a physical altercation that led to death."

"But that still doesn't narrow it down enough for us. Whatever the means of death, the injuries could have been internal."

"That's correct. We won't know until we're able to better examine these bones."

Another thought slammed into Cassidy's mind. "I wonder if these bones are connected with the bone that Carter Denver's dog brought home a few weeks ago."

The bone had been sent off for testing, but they didn't have the results back yet. Cassidy felt certain it was human, but only a specialist could say for sure. The bone hadn't been at the top of the state lab's to-do list.

"I'd say there's a good chance," Clemson said. "One of the victims is missing a humerus."

Cassidy pressed her lips together as she looked at their little cemetery, this one without a neat and tidy fence around it. No, this one was cordoned off with crime-scene tape. Instead of beautiful flower arrangements and headstones, there were ragged tree stumps and unruly weeds.

It was a shame that death had taken away a person's dignity.

No, she vowed. Cassidy would find out who these people were. What had happened to them. They would get their justice.

As the promise echoed in Cassidy's mind, the sound of a boat drew her attention. Had one of the agencies sent their guys here via the water? How strange.

But as she tried to get a better look at the boat, she frowned. The vessel didn't appear to be a police boat. There were no markings to indicate that. No, it looked like a run-of-the-mill skiff.

"Do you think the media got hold of this already?" Doc Clemson raised his hand over his eyes to block the glaring sun.

"I can't imagine . . ."

Just as the words left Cassidy's lips, a sound ripped through the air.

Gunfire.

Someone was shooting at them, she realized.

CHAPTER FOUR

CASSIDY THREW herself over Doc Clemson, and they hit the sand just as a bullet splintered the tree beside them.

"Leggott! Dane!" Cassidy yelled. "Get down!"

Her officers dove to the ground.

When she knew they were safe, Cassidy glanced over at the water. The men aboard the skiff fired again.

A bullet hit the ground near Cassidy, sending pellets of sand flying into her face.

Her heart raced.

These guys were shooting to kill.

She drew her gun, knowing it would be difficult to get a clear shot from her vantage point.

Just as she raised her weapon, the boat sped away, with two men wearing ball caps and sunglasses on board.

"Everyone okay?" Cassidy yelled.

Everyone murmured back that they were.

Cassidy rolled off Clemson and stood. Her heart still raced from the encounter.

She helped Clemson to his feet then pulled out her phone and called the Coast Guard and marine police, asking them to be on the lookout for the watercraft. But Cassidy's gut told her the officials wouldn't find those two men. By the time they deployed their boats, the gunmen would be gone.

The boat had been too far away to allow her to see any type of identifiable markers—anything to distinguish the men or the boat. She could only hope the men would slip up and be discovered.

She glanced at her crew as they gathered near her and confirmed with her own eyes that no one had been injured.

Good. That was the important thing.

Gunmen firing on them was the last thing she'd expected at this scene.

"While we're here, we're going to need to keep guard, just in case anyone attempts any other shenanigans like that," Cassidy started. "Leggott, you take the first watch. Dane, I need you to retrieve the bullets out of the trees and sand and document them. We'll see if they match anything we have on file."

"And me?" Clemson's voice held a new tremble.

"You just keep working for these victims," Cassidy said. "We'll keep a lookout around you to make sure nothing like that happens again."

"Sounds good."

Cassidy took a step away, still surveying everything around her for any signs of trouble. Those men had to be associated in some way with these remains. Somehow, they had learned that these bodies had been discovered. They'd come here trying to silence Cassidy and her team.

But how? How had they been privy to this information?

Nothing had been on the police scanner. No, Leggott had called Cassidy and asked her to come.

The only people who knew about this were Cassidy, Wayne, the other law enforcement agencies she'd called in, and the mayor. Had one of them spilled the beans?

She glanced around, her gaze stopping on Leggott as he stood on the shore, keeping watch over the water just as directed.

Cassidy *had* seen Leggott on his phone with someone about a half hour ago.

He wouldn't have shared this information, would he?

The bad feeling in her gut grew. She didn't want to think anyone she knew would be that irresponsible. Or even worse—what if someone had shared the information knowing she and everyone else out here could have been killed? Could someone Cassidy trusted be that ruthless?

Just then, her phone rang, jerking her from her thoughts.

Cassidy pulled the device from her pocket but hesitated before looking at the screen.

What if it was another message? Another indication from someone that Cassidy had been made?

A sickly feeling trickled into her gut as she glanced at the screen.

She released her breath.

It wasn't another threat. No, it was her friend Skye.

Cassidy put the phone to her ear. "What's up, girl?"

"Cassidy, it's Serena." Skye's words ran together and her pitch escalated.

Serena was Skye's college-aged niece who lived here on the island with her. Cassidy's stomach clenched with anticipation. "What's wrong?"

"She's gone."

Cassidy stepped away from any listening ears. "Skye, what do you mean by 'she's gone'?"

"I mean, Serena left her ice cream truck at my place. Her car is still here. She even left her cell phone. I've been trying to find her for the last three hours, but she's nowhere."

Cassidy didn't want to ask the questions that came to mind. She didn't want to face what she knew was most likely the truth. But she had to know more details.

"I know that's strange, but those things don't necessarily mean Serena is *gone* gone. Maybe she's just at a friend's house. Serena isn't always the most responsible person."

"No one has seen her, Cassidy." Skye's voice

cracked. "The last I knew, she was with Dietrich. I think . . . I think Serena may have gone with him to Gilead's Cove."

"What?" Cassidy's dread turned into all-out anxiety.

That was the worst-case scenario she'd feared. Gilead's Cove was the name of a community here on the island, an old campground and RV park that had been purchased by a charismatic man named Anthony Gilead several months ago.

No one knew exactly what went on behind those fences, but Cassidy knew enough to realize it was not good. The people there were a part of a cult, most likely. Even worse, the group had begun to buy up additional properties on the island, which she could only guess meant they were trying to expand.

Dietrich was one of Gilead's righthand men. The twentysomething man was good-looking, and he'd set his sights on Serena recently. Cassidy trusted him with Serena just about as much as she trusted the weatherman to give an accurate forecast.

"It's true," Skye said. "Serena is gone. I . . . I don't know what to do. Can you help me? Please."

Cassidy glanced around. Saw Clemson documenting the bodies. Saw her officers guarding the scene.

She couldn't leave right now. There was just no way. But Cassidy desperately wanted to help her friend out.

"Hold tight, okay? I'll come to your place as soon as

I can. Whatever you do, don't try to go to Gilead's Cove alone, okay?"

"But I need to get Serena out of there before they make her one of them! Before they brainwash her and change her into someone I don't even know anymore."

"I understand. I really do. But those people won't let you beyond their gates. I'm at a scene right now that I can't leave, but I will as soon as possible. Promise me you won't do anything without me."

Skye said nothing.

"Skye . . ." Cassidy warned, fearing her friend would do something rash that would end in more heartache.

"Okay, I won't."

But as Cassidy hung up the phone, the unsettled feeling in her stomach remained. What had Serena gotten herself into? And the even scarier question: Would Cassidy truly be able to help?

AGENT GABE ABBOTT with the NCSBI arrived on the scene an hour later. He'd been staying on the island on and off since this area had become part of his district, but he happened to be up north today. It had taken him longer to get here than Cassidy anticipated.

After Cassidy explained the situation to him, she called in Mac, who was not only her friend but the former police chief and a current mayoral candidate. He and Ty had been sworn in as officers of the law during the last case, and now they both could serve as auxiliary officers when needed.

Mac came to the scene to keep an eye on things for her. She trusted his judgment and knew he'd be on the lookout for trouble.

The truth was that it would be hours—days—maybe even weeks before they had any answers as to who these victims were.

As much as Cassidy might want to remain on the scene, she knew there were other things here on this island that needed to be done. All of their resources couldn't remain here indefinitely.

Cassidy's first priority was to go check on Skye and to look for Serena.

The thought of Serena becoming a part of Gilead's Cove . . . it was enough to make Cassidy sick to her stomach. Serena was different, to put it mildly. She was quirky and unique and boy crazy. She defined a person who was trying to find herself with her ever-changing personalities and wardrobes and jobs.

But she was smarter than this. Smart enough to know not to step foot inside that compound . . . right?

Please, Lord. Let her be smarter than that . . .

Five minutes later, Cassidy pulled to a stop in front of Skye's home. Skye lived in a retro RV she kept parked at a local campground—the island's alternative to affordable housing.

Cassidy threw her SUV into Park before hopping

out and hurrying up the steps to a small but welcoming deck, complete with a colorful hammock, a cheerful rug, and soothing windchimes.

Before she could even knock, Skye threw the door open. Her eyes were red-rimmed and watery as she leaned outside, her long, lean limbs looking taut with stress.

Skye had obviously been crying.

Cassidy pulled her into a hug. "Oh, sweetie. I'm so sorry."

"I can't believe she would do this." Skye sniffled, nearly going limp in Cassidy's arms.

"Let's go inside and talk." Cassidy took her elbow and directed her back into the RV. Austin—Skye's boyfriend—sat on the couch there, looking as exhausted and worried as Cassidy felt.

When they were all seated, Cassidy leaned toward Skye. "Have you heard from Serena since we spoke?"

Skye swung her head back and forth. "No, nothing. I have no way of getting in touch. Her phone is here. But I called all her friends, and no one has talked to her today."

"Did you call Dietrich?"

Skye shook her head. "No, I don't have his number. But you know Serena. She never leaves home without her phone. That's a huge red flag within itself."

Cassidy couldn't argue. "I know this sounds intrusive, but have you checked Serena's phone for any messages? Normally, it would be off-limits, but in this case—"

"I don't know her passcode," Skye blurted, "or I would have. Normally, I'm against stuff like that too and think people deserve their privacy. But not right now. Not when I think Serena may have made the biggest mistake of her life and she may be in danger."

Cassidy shifted as Skye's words echoed throughout the room. *Danger.* Yes, that was the word Cassidy had been thinking about also. The one she hadn't wanted to voice aloud.

"Has she been hanging out with Dietrich a lot?" Cassidy hadn't talked to Serena in a few days and didn't want to make too many assumptions. Cassidy had warned the girl to stay away from the man.

Skye nodded. "I think so. I mean, Serena knew I didn't approve, so she wasn't telling me. But I strongly suspect she was spending a lot of time with Dietrich behind my back."

"He has a house outside the compound, right?"

"That's what I heard. I don't know where."

"I can find out." Cassidy stood, a new mission in mind.

"Are you going to go there?" Skye's tear-stained gaze looked up at her, a faint glimmer of hope appearing.

"You know it."

"Let me go with you." Skye jumped to her feet.

"It would be better if you stayed here with Austin."

Cassidy's gaze locked with Austin, and he nodded, getting Cassidy's subtle hint.

"She's right, Skye," Austin encouraged. "Let Cassidy check this out first. If she needs us, she'll call us."

"You promise?" Skye clutched Cassidy's arm with such force that Cassidy nearly flinched.

"I promise, Skye." Cassidy paused, thinking through the possibilities of what might play out over the next several hours. "Is there any reason to think Serena didn't go of her own free will into that compound?"

Skye stared at her, eyes wide and damp. "No, why?"

Cassidy bit down. "Just asking. I'll be in touch."

But Cassidy knew that if Serena went into Gilead's Cove of her own volition it would be nearly impossible to get her out. But she didn't think that was news that Skye could handle right now.

CHAPTER FIVE

AS TY WAITED on the driveway beneath his house, he popped a tennis ball belonging to his dog, Kujo, against the shed wall. Somehow the motion helped him to sort his thoughts.

After finding that camera, he and Braden had spent the rest of the morning searching the cottage. They'd found two other cameras—one in the kitchen and another outside.

Ty had collected them, hoping they might reveal something about the person who'd planted the devices there. But he didn't have much hope. The devices were high tech, which signaled to him that whoever had left them was no amateur.

Could it be someone from his past as a SEAL? One of the enemies he'd made while on the job? Or did this have to do with Cassidy—with her background in Seattle? For all Ty knew, the hidden devices could even tie in with something that had happened here on the island.

He didn't know, and he didn't like not knowing.

Ty hadn't told Cassidy about the cameras yet. The fact that she'd been occupied all morning meant that she'd been called to another big case. He would tell her when the time was right.

Just like he'd tell her about his financial worries concerning Hope House when the opportunity arose.

Both of those facts, when combined, made defeat press on his shoulders. Not only did Ty feel like he was failing when it came to keeping Cassidy safe, but then he also felt the sting of unspoken expectations. They weren't expectations Cassidy had put on him—they were expectations he'd put on himself.

Expectations that he would be the breadwinner and support his family financially. He knew it sounded macho, but it was the way he'd been raised. He'd been taught to work hard and to take care of the people he loved.

But as he'd been crunching numbers for Hope House, he'd realized that those numbers weren't good enough. He needed to start doing more fundraising for the nonprofit. After some flooding earlier in the year, which required repairs, his surplus of cash had dried up.

Paying for the travel expenses of those coming to the retreat center was important to him. He didn't want the experience to be a financial burden but a blessing. But the operating costs were more significant than Ty had anticipated, and now he had to find more money or cancel his next session.

He hadn't told Cassidy about that. She'd had so much on her mind lately that Ty didn't want to stress her out any more than absolutely necessary. But they'd have to have some hard conversations soon.

He bounced the tennis ball against the shed once more, caught it, and bounced it back again. A few repetitions later, Cassidy's SUV pulled up. He discarded the ball into a bin by the shed door and then climbed in beside Cassidy, giving her a quick kiss on the cheek.

"Good afternoon, beautiful," he murmured.

"Good afternoon."

Cassidy had called him ten minutes ago and asked if he wanted to help her look into Serena's supposed disappearance. Of course, Ty had said yes—especially since he assumed her disappearance could be connected with Gilead's Cove.

Ty had made Cassidy promise she wouldn't go to that place alone. Everything about the compound gave him the creeps—especially the way Anthony Gilead looked at Cassidy.

There was more to the man than met the eye. Ty just had to figure out what.

Ty stretched his arm against the back of the seat as they started down the road. "How's Skye?"

Cassidy frowned. "Devastated. Upset. Freaked out. Everything you can imagine."

"I can't believe Serena would do this. Yet, at the same time, I guess I can. I've never quite understood the way that girl thinks."

Serena was prone to dressing like a different personality every day. One day she might look like Pippi Longstocking, another day she might dress like a politician, and yet a different day she might don an urban look dressed like a hip-hop star.

What the girl lacked in common sense she made up for in enthusiasm. Still, she made Ty's head spin.

Cassidy's gaze looked intense and focused as she stared at the road. "You know, Serena said something to me a while ago that's been bugging me ever since. I had mentioned maybe we should send a spy into Gilead's Cove. She overheard and volunteered."

Ty sucked in a quick breath. "That sounds like a terrible idea."

"I agree. I told her under no conditions would she do something like that." Cassidy stole a glance at him, her gaze softening. "I'm afraid she had other ideas, Ty."

He rubbed his chin as his thoughts churned inside him. "Or even worse—what if Serena really wants to be a part of this community, Cassidy?"

Cassidy frowned. "I can't even go there. If Serena is there because she wants to be there . . . then we've lost her. If she's there because she wants to be a hero . . . then she's in more danger than she can possibly realize. If she's caught—well, I can't even think about it."

Ty couldn't agree more. His chest squeezed with

tension at the thought. "Let's just hope Dietrich has some answers for us."

"Let's hope." Cassidy glanced at him again. "It's been an interesting morning."

"What's going on?" Ty figured it was something big since Cassidy had been gone all day.

She told him about the discovery of the three skeletons in the woods, as well as about the men on the boat who'd shot at the crime-scene crew. For such a small island, this place had more than its fair share of mysteries and crimes. Ty wasn't sure how he felt about that.

"Someone just dumped these people's remains there, Ty," Cassidy finished. "Like they were trash or something. No grave markings. Nothing."

He reached over and squeezed her knee, hearing the disbelief in her voice. One of the reasons Cassidy was so good at her job was because she actually cared about people. She channeled her compassion into a drive to find answers.

"I know," he murmured. "There's a lot of things you see in police work—a lot of things I saw being a SEAL —that you can never unsee."

"I realize you understand that just as well as anyone." Cassidy let out a sigh before continuing, "We're guessing that those bodies have only been there for three or four months."

As soon as Cassidy repeated the timeline, Ty knew exactly what she was alluding to. "Which would be about the time Gilead's Cove came into town."

"Exactly." Her voice sounded stony, with equal parts resolve and disgust.

"So you think they're connected?"

Cassidy shrugged and let out a sigh. "I have no idea. I know I don't trust Anthony Gilead. I think his followers are like zombies who will do whatever he wants. And I don't have enough evidence to prove he's guilty of anything, so I'm helpless to stop him."

"What about Lela?" Ty asked. "Has she talked yet?"

Lela Walker had been married to Anthony Gilead, but she'd fled the relationship. Cassidy had hoped to get information from her, but Gilead had gotten to the woman before the police could. Now she refused to say anything about Gilead's Cove. She'd been their best hope for getting answers.

Ty and Cassidy both suspected that Gilead had threatened Lela with her brother's life if she spoke to anyone. Her brother, Kaleb Walker, was still a member of the cult. And, so far, she'd held true. She hadn't muttered a thing about the cult—as far as Ty knew, at least.

"No, Lela hasn't said a single word," Cassidy confirmed.

"That's unfortunate. No doubt Lela could have brought the whole group down."

"I agree." Cassidy stared straight ahead as she drove toward the other end of the island. "There's one more thing. The only people who knew that these bodies had been discovered were law enforcement and the fisherman who found the skeletons."

"Okay . . ."

"Someone on my team must have told someone what was going on. Otherwise, how did those gunmen know we were there? Know that we'd found the skeletons when we did?"

Ty's breath hitched. "You think you have a snitch within the department?"

"It's hard to say for sure, but I think it's a possibility." Cassidy sounded grim as she spoke the words, as if the realization burdened her—and it should. In police work, you had to trust your team. Your life depended on it. It was the same as being a SEAL.

"If that's true then everything you say and do could possibly be reported back to an enemy." Ty didn't like the thought of that. Not one bit. The situation was precarious enough without adding a spy to the mix.

"I know. Believe me, I know." Cassidy pulled up to a beach box-style house and put the vehicle into Park. "Let's just hope that Dietrich has some answers for us."

Ty hoped he did. But the realistic side of him knew this wouldn't be an easy conversation.

———

CASSIDY POUNDED on the door to Dietrich's place and waited. A car had been parked outside the house, so she assumed Dietrich was here. Yet, if he wasn't, that could give her an excuse to visit Gilead's Cove again.

Dietrich answered a few minutes later, tugging his earbuds out and offering a smile.

The man was probably Cassidy's age—in his late twenties. He had dirty blond hair with spikes, blue eyes, and a slight but muscular build. In his athletic shorts and damp T-shirt, he looked like he'd just gotten back from jogging.

"Chief Chambers." Dietrich's gaze flipped behind her to Ty, and he nodded a polite greeting before looking back at Cassidy. "To what do I owe the honor of this visit?"

Cassidy's stomach churned. This guy might want to appear charming and like the boy next door, but she knew better. He would do Gilead's bidding, no matter the cost.

"Have you seen Serena today?" Cassidy skipped the small talk.

Dietrich hesitated before nodding slowly. "I have. Why? Is everything okay?"

Cassidy's hands went to her hips. "Where is she? We're all worried about her."

"There's nothing to be worried about. Serena is finally finding her place in this world. She's been struggling with knowing who she really is for a long time, as you probably know, but—"

"Where is she?" Cassidy interrupted.

Dietrich's smile faded, and he squared his shoulders. "She's at Gilead's Cove, of course."

"I want to talk to her."

"That's up to Serena."

"This isn't a game, Dietrich." Cassidy could barely keep the anger out of her voice. "I need to talk to Serena. Now. Face-to-face."

He stepped closer. "Chief, Serena willingly decided to move to Gilead's Cove. There's nothing illegal going on here. She's a grown woman who's made her own choices. Even though those choices might be different from what you would have chosen, that doesn't mean they're wrong—"

"Spare me the lecture," Cassidy said. "I won't believe she's okay and that she did this on her own until I speak with her. Until then, I consider you a suspect in her abduction."

His gaze darkened. "There's been no abducting here."

"Then you'll need to prove that. Serena told no one what she was doing."

"Because she knew no one would approve. She felt like she had no choice but to do this in secret."

Cassidy fisted her hands as anger, and anxiety collided inside her. "I meant what I said, Dietrich. I need to speak with her. Do I need to take you down to the station? Because I can arrange that. Easily."

His eyes narrowed. "No, you don't. Let me talk to her first."

"You have two hours. Otherwise, I'm getting a warrant. Do you understand?"

"I understand."

Just as Cassidy stepped away, her phone buzzed. It was Leggott. They'd found something else at the crime scene.

It looked like she'd need to wait before telling Ty about that text she'd received this morning. She needed to tell him when they had a moment they could talk—really talk.

In the meantime, Cassidy would continue to keep her eyes open for any signs of trouble.

CHAPTER SIX

"WHAT DOES fishing line have to do with this?" Back at the crime scene after dropping Ty off, Cassidy stared at Mac and Leggott as she waited for a reasonable explanation.

The NCSBI crew worked in the woods. They'd laid down tarps, donned hazmat suits, and had begun to carefully work the bodies. The scene reminded Cassidy of an excavation site.

The cold wind that swept over the island had brought with it a new gift—the smell of decaying eel grass that had been pushed ashore. The plant rotted in the sunlight, and the wind spread its scent all over the shore.

Cassidy, Mac, Clemson, and Leggott had moved farther down the beach for some privacy. The crashing waves concealed their words as the lighthouse in the distance stood guard over their conversation.

It wasn't that the Lantern Beach PD was on the opposing side of the NCSBI. But a particularly tense case had recently pitted Cassidy against Agent Abbott, and now she felt certain she needed to maintain her distance until she figured out if the man was a friend or a foe.

Mac MacArthur held up his phone, where he'd taken some photos. The man was in his late sixties, but he carried himself like someone much younger. He kept his white hair, mustache and goatee neat and trimmed. Likewise, his physique.

"It's not the fishing line," Mac explained. "It's the sinker at the end of the fishing line."

Cassidy stared at the metal piece in the photo. It had been shaped to look like an anchor. "What about the sinker is important?"

She knew she was missing something—she just wasn't sure what.

"Isaac Warsaw makes these and sells them on the island," Leggott explained. "He has for years. They're his signature product. Not many sinkers look like anchors."

"Okay, but if Isaac sells these, anyone could have bought three," Cassidy said. "It doesn't necessarily point back to Isaac."

"The line was found wrapped around the victims' necks," Mac continued. "With the same sinker on the end of each."

She sucked in a quick breath. "Do you think that's

how these people died? Were they strangled with fishing line?"

Everyone turned toward Clemson, who cringed. "It's too early to say. I have trouble believing it, however. While it's possible, I can't see someone adding a sinker to each line only to strangle three different people."

"So you think maybe this was planted here as evidence?" Cassidy said.

"I think it's a good guess."

"It sounds like I need to go talk to Isaac." Cassidy had never talked to the man, but she'd heard plenty of stories about him.

He lived in an old shack near the water and spent most of his time fishing and gardening—so much so that he hardly ever had to interact with the regular world. In fact, the couple times Cassidy had seen Isaac in town, his dark hair had looked greasy and his clothes had smelled like he hadn't changed them in a while.

Cassidy supposed more could be going on in that secluded fishing cabin than anyone suspected. Being on the water, there was a lot of space for privacy, for illegal exchanges and transactions.

"Let me see what I can find out," Cassidy said.

At least, it was *something*. It gave her some direction to search. She'd take that over nothing.

Cassidy wandered back to Agent Abbott, who'd taken over the scene. It hadn't been a surprise. The man seemed like a team player on the outside. But Cassidy had caught glimpses of the fact that he liked his power and control.

Ever since their last case, she hadn't cared for the man that much. Maybe it was because he'd stepped on her toes. Or maybe it was because he was difficult. It was hard to say.

"How's it going?" Cassidy's voice took on a more professional tone, one that aimed to keep distance from Abbott and his power plays.

The short, stout man with an oversized square face and balding head glanced up at her. He seemed to share her sentiments—that the two of them were best off if they kept each other at arm's distance.

"We'll be here a while," Abbott said. "After we document the scene, we'll take the bones back to the crime lab in Raleigh and process them there. Hopefully, we can make some IDs and figure out what happened to these people."

"Until we know who they are, it's going to be hard to make any kind of case."

"Exactly. We don't know if this is a crime scene or if these people were peacefully—but illegally—buried here. We'll scour missing persons reports, of course."

Cassidy studied his face, wondering if he'd discovered anything he hadn't shared. "Anything I need to know?"

"Not yet." His words held almost an icy edge to them, as if warning Cassidy not to overstep her boundaries. "You?"

"I heard about the fishing line."

"Know anything about it?"

"I might have a lead. You mind if I check it out? A local may have made those sinkers."

"Just let me know what you learn." He paused. "Please."

"Of course. If I'm done here, I'll leave your crew to continue working," Cassidy said. "Leggott is going to remain here and keep the scene secure. Let me know if you need anything else."

"Will do."

Cassidy could feel Abbott's gaze on her as she walked away.

She was going to go talk to Isaac Warsaw and see what he knew. She hoped the answers might come easily, but she was smart enough to know that things were rarely ever easy.

———

SINCE TY WAS BACK at work—he'd told Cassidy he had to do some paperwork for Hope House—Cassidy took Dane with her to talk to Isaac. Dane was their newest officer here in Lantern Beach. He had proven, along with his dog, Ranger, to be an asset to the department.

But Cassidy's thoughts wandered back to her earlier realization that someone in her circle might be a snitch for Gilead's Cove. Could it be Dane?

Dane was from Cincinnati. What was that? A three-hour drive to West Virginia? Did he have roots there, maybe?

Then again, Leggott had called in sick because of his asthma. What if that was a cover for something else?

Cassidy shook her head. She didn't want to think like this. Didn't want to think that someone she trusted could be loyal to the other side.

But she understood how it all worked. She'd gone undercover and infiltrated a deadly gang when she was a detective in Seattle. No one had a clue she was actually an undercover officer. Her purpose had been to blend in, to obtain information, and to report it.

At the memory, she recalled the text message she'd gotten earlier. Had someone from her past found her here? Was this person watching her every move now? Had they shot at her earlier?

She didn't know, but she didn't like any of this.

She would need to remain cautious and guarded, for more than one reason.

Cassidy pulled down a long, narrow road surrounded by trees and clumps of broken concrete. Isaac's residence wasn't terribly far from the lighthouse beach.

Did that mean anything? Cassidy didn't know. But she stored that fact in the back of her mind, just in case.

A small house appeared at the end of the lane. Cedar shingles were missing from the sides, trash had collected in every crevice, and large items like tires, broken bicycles, and cracked chairs littered the rest of the space.

A lone figure with a fishing pole sat on a rickety-looking pier behind the residence. Isaac Warsaw.

Cassidy and Dane started toward him. The man didn't turn or flinch. He just held his fishing pole and stared out at the water.

Even when Cassidy stopped directly beside him, he didn't look.

"Mr. Warsaw," she started.

He remained staring straight ahead. "How can I help you, Chief?"

She repressed a shudder, wondering how the man knew it was her without ever turning his head. She'd been watching him. "I have some questions I was hoping you could answer for me."

"I reckon I can give it a shot—long as it doesn't stop the fish from biting."

She edged herself forward, trying to get a better look at his face. "Mr. Warsaw, you make fishing sinkers that look like this, correct?"

She found the photo on her phone and shoved it in front of the man.

He turned his eyes from the water for long enough to stare at her screen. "That's correct."

"Where do you sell them?"

"Only one place—the tackle shop in town. Moby Rick's."

"No one ever buys them from you personally?"

"No, ma'am. If you can't tell, I'm not too good with people. Prefer just to fish."

"You don't remember anyone who's bought the sinkers from you then? Anyone who may have bought multiple ones?"

"No, can't say I do. Maybe Moby will know more. I'd talk to him. I don't sell direct. Don't like working with people."

Cassidy shoved her phone back in her pocket. She wasn't getting very far here. But she'd known it would be too good to be true if she could find some answers this easily. "Thanks for your time."

As she started to walk away, Isaac called to her. Cassidy pivoted toward him.

He'd actually looked away from the water and faced her. The lines of his face were illuminated by the sinking sun and made him look even older than he already did.

"Yes?" she said.

"I don't know anything about those skeletons."

Her back tightened, and she glanced at Dane. He seemed to share her sentiments. Normal people didn't say stuff like that—especially considering that Cassidy hadn't mentioned anything about skeletons.

She shifted. "Why would you say that, Isaac?"

"I got the pictures."

"What pictures?"

"The ones someone slipped beneath my door."

Cassidy shook her head, unsure if she was understanding this correctly. "What photos did someone slip beneath your door, Isaac?"

"Photos of three skeletons with my sinkers around their necks."

Realization washed over her like a nuclear aftermath. "Isaac, when did you get these photos, and why didn't you tell the police about them?"

"They weren't real skeletons. Just a joke."

"They were real, Isaac. You need to start talking."

"Someone sent me some pictures about a month ago. Slipped them under my door. I thought it was a prank. Some of those skeletons like the Doc used down at the clinic, only doctored up with some leftover Halloween makeup or something. Nothing real."

Cassidy's jaw clenched. "You should have reported it, Isaac. "

"I just want to be left alone. And I thought it was a joke."

"Do you still have the photos?"

He lifted a shoulder. "As a matter of fact, I do. I don't like throwing things away."

Cassidy sighed. "I need to see them. Now."

"Okay. As soon as I bring this one in." As he said the words, something tugged on his line, and he began spinning his reel until an eight-inch fish popped out of the water.

Only in Lantern Beach, Cassidy thought to herself. Only in Lantern Beach.

CHAPTER SEVEN

STILL STANDING outside Isaac's cottage, Cassidy stared at the glossy 4x6 photos. There were five pictures. Each showed the victims—the skeletons—with fishing line near their clavicle.

Three of the photos highlighted three individual corpses, and the last two photos were views of all the victims together in the woods.

Strangely enough, the bodies weren't covered with sand. Did that mean they'd never been hidden in the sand? Had they not been buried at all?

Cassidy squinted as she studied the photos. One of the images was taken from a different angle—from inside the woods. It showed not only the bodies, but also the water beyond it. In the background, she could see the ferry bringing people to and from the island.

Those passengers probably had no clue what was going on over on the seemingly peaceful shores.

"What do you think?" Dane asked, looking over her shoulder.

"I don't even know what to think about this." Cassidy glanced at Isaac, trying to read his body language.

He worked a knot out of one of his fishing lines as he stood there, but otherwise he looked placid—not guilty, not flustered, not even curious. Just imperturbable.

"There was no note or anything else with this?" Cassidy continued. "Just photos?"

Isaac nodded slowly, continuing to work out his line. "That's right."

"And you have no idea who left them?" Cassidy continued.

"No idea. I figured someone wanted to spook me."

Cassidy felt her impatience growing at his lack of focus on the conversation. She took a deep breath to temper her words. "Any idea who would want to do that or why?"

"Nope. I leave people alone. Made no sense. Like I said earlier, I figured it was a joke." He released his line, seemingly satisfied he'd gotten the knot out.

"That's a pretty extravagant joke." Cassidy watched his expression again, trying to get a read on whether or not he actually believed his own words. He didn't flinch or twitch—there was no sign he was trying to be deceitful.

"I just want to leave people alone," Isaac said. "I want to live my life and let other people live theirs."

Cassidy wasn't going to get anything else from him. Not right now, at least. "We're going to have to take these in for evidence, Isaac."

"Please do. I don't want them photos anymore."

"And I'm going to have to ask you to stay in town," Cassidy said.

He glanced over at her, the first hint of amusement in his gaze. "Chief, I haven't left this island in thirty years. I don't plan on leaving now."

"Good to know. Take care, Isaac."

But Cassidy felt even more confused now than she had earlier. Why in the world would someone give Isaac these photos? What would they hope to prove?

As soon as she got into her car, her phone buzzed. She put the phone to her ear, not recognizing the number.

"Serena doesn't want to talk to you," someone said.

Dietrich. Dietrich had called her, just as he said he would.

"What do you mean she doesn't want to talk to me?" Cassidy asked. "I need to hear that for myself. I told you that, Dietrich. Otherwise, I have no choice but to think you abducted her."

"That's asinine," he retorted, a sharp edge to his voice. "Of course, I didn't abduct her."

"I need to hear that from Serena."

He said nothing for a moment then, "She'll call you later."

"She'd better."

"She will."

But as Cassidy hung up, her unease grew. Too many things were going wrong. Way too many things at one time.

————

ON THE WAY back to the scene, Cassidy and Dane swung by Moby Rick's. Apparently, that was the man's real name, and his mother had a killer sense of humor. Even more ironic was the fact that he had opened a tackle shop.

Cassidy had met him once before, and the man, in his late twenties, seemed to have a similar personality to Isaac. He liked to keep to himself and preferred to spend time with fish rather than people.

She asked him about the sinkers. The man was almost as much help as Isaac had been. He didn't remember anyone buying them in bulk and couldn't remember anything strange about the product. He promised to call if he thought of anything, though.

Cassidy headed back to the lighthouse beach and joined Abbott there. She had two hours until Lisa and Braden's wedding shower at the church. She'd promised to attend and didn't want to let her friends down. Police work was important, but it couldn't consume her entire life.

She paused on the sandy beach, watching as the sun set behind the scene. The peaceful colors were a stark contrast to the grisly cemetery they'd found. Abbott's team was still there, still in their hazmat suits, and still working to collect the bodies without damaging them.

Abbott scowled when he saw Cassidy and moseyed toward her. "You came back."

"Of course I did." She gave him the update on the sinkers and handed him the photos, finishing with, "How about you? Anything new?"

He shook his head. "No, nothing at all. Hopefully we'll know more soon. It's hard to even search missing persons reports until we know the age of the victims."

"Makes sense."

Abbott paused and studied Cassidy a moment before saying, "The mayor came out here and asked for you."

Cassidy bristled. "Did he?"

"I told him that we'd be handling the case."

Cassidy was sure that Tomlinson had loved that answer. "Got it."

"We should be wrapping up here in about an hour. We've gone through everything."

"And you didn't find any clues?"

"Nothing that seems to mean anything. Not yet, at least."

"I am the police chief on the island, so I expect you'll keep me updated."

He scowled. "Of course."

"Will you be staying in town?"

"No, I'll be traveling with the remains to Raleigh. But I'll be back as needed."

"Of course."

"And if you hear anything, I expect that you'll share that information with me."

"It's only professional."

The two exchanged frosty nods. Despite their differences, they had a lot of work to do to bring justice to the victims they'd discovered today.

CHAPTER EIGHT

CASSIDY ARRIVED at Lisa and Braden's wedding shower ten minutes late. But the important thing was that she'd arrived. After leaving Abbott, she'd gone to the station to write reports about today's discovery.

Ty had saved a seat beside him in the semi-circle in the fellowship hall of the community church. And it was a good thing because it looked like half the town had turned out for the event.

"Everything okay?" Ty whispered, his breath rushing across her cheek.

Cassidy nodded, flashing a smile at another couple a few seats down. She still wore her police uniform. She hadn't had time to go home and change, and she felt out of place as police chief right now.

"It was a long day," Cassidy muttered, glancing around.

Lisa and Braden sat in the center, facing the semi-circle, both smiling and looking happier than ever as they opened gifts and marveled at their new towels and plates.

Skye scooted into the seat beside Cassidy, her eyes still red with tears as she whispered, "Did you hear anything?"

Cassidy glanced around again, trying not to draw any attention to the conversation. Finally, she took Skye's hand. "Let's go to the bathroom."

Cassidy stepped from the fellowship hall and into a dark hallway lined with bathrooms and several Sunday school classrooms. She paused there and gripped Skye's hand.

"I talked to Dietrich earlier," Cassidy explained. "Twice for that matter. Serena is supposed to call later."

She filled her friend in on the rest of the story.

"So, he's saying Serena joined Gilead's Cove willing-ly?" Skye's voice sounded thin enough to break.

"That's what Dietrich said. We'll talk to Serena. We need to hear it from her own lips."

"Can't you just go get her? Force her to go home?"

Cassidy wished that were the case. "Not if Serena went willingly. She's an adult. If she wants to go join a cult, she's allowed to do just that."

Skye squeezed the skin between her eyes. "Cassidy, if Serena joins Gilead's Cove, I may never see her alive again."

The pit in Cassidy's stomach grew. Her friend's

words were true. These people were dangerous. Maybe even deadly.

"We're going to figure this out," Cassidy murmured. "No one stands alone, remember?"

It was the theme of their Bible study, and Cassidy had clung to that mantra many times. Her friends had been there for her and even put their lives on the line to save Cassidy. They were like the family she'd always wanted.

As if on cue, Cassidy's phone rang. It was Dietrich's number.

She stepped farther into the darkness and motioned for Skye to follow. Quickly, she put her phone to her ear, anxious to hear what he had to say.

"Hello?" Cassidy rushed.

"It's me," a female voice said with a flat, unenthusiastic tone.

"Serena?" Cassidy glanced at Skye, and her friend leaned in closer so she could hear also. "Where are you?"

"I'm at Gilead's Cove," Serena said. "You don't have to worry about me."

"Serena, we are worried about you." Skye reached for the phone and pulled it closer. "You need to come home. Now. I told your mom I would take care of you. What are you thinking?"

"Aunt Skye, I'm fine. Gilead's Cove is a peaceful group. We're all about love and acceptance." Serena's voice lacked her normal enthusiasm, but she didn't sound scared. No, more matter of fact than anything.

"Serena—" Skye started.

Cassidy raised a hand. They didn't have much time, and she couldn't let Skye fuss at her for the entire conversation. That would get them nowhere.

"Skye, did you go to Gilead's Cove willingly?" Cassidy's heart thumped as she waited for an answer. She desperately wanted the girl to say no. She wanted an excuse to go get her, to know she was safe and to maybe even bring this group down.

"Of course I did," Serena said. "Did you really think Dietrich abducted me? He's actually a really nice guy. If you got to know him, you'd see that."

Serena's monotone almost took on a bitter edge. The tone didn't even sound like Serena. The girl had more personality than anyone Cassidy had ever met—and she was always happy and perky.

"Serena, there's more to these people than meets the eye," Cassidy continued. "Can't you consider this a little more? A little longer?"

"I've been thinking about it for a while, but I knew no one would approve. This is where I want to be. I'm sorry it's not what you want, Aunt Skye. But in my gut, I know this is right. It's time for some changes in my life. It's time for me to grow up. Haven't you told me that before? That I was immature?"

"You know this isn't what I meant!" Skye's voice cracked. "You can't twist my words like that."

"I'm not twisting them," Serena said. "That's what you said. I listened to your advice."

Skye started to respond, but Cassidy urged her to stay quiet another moment. "Serena, we can talk about this later. Right now, I'd really like to see you face-to-face. I want to see your eyes so I can know this is legit."

"Not right now."

"Serena, for all I know, someone could be holding a gun to your head and forcing you to say this," Cassidy said.

"They're not. I promise. I'm okay. But I can't see you right now."

Impatience clenched at Cassidy's spine. "Then when?"

"I . . . I don't know. I need more time, I guess."

"Because they won't let you leave, will they?" Skye yelled into the phone.

Cassidy glanced behind her, wondering if their voices had carried into the wedding shower. She put her hand on Skye's arm and squeezed, trying to get her to calm down.

"That's not true," Serena said. "But we value privacy. Now, I really need to go—"

"Serena, don't you get off this phone," Skye yelled. "I need you back. You can't stay."

"You're wrong. This is my choice."

"Serena—"

But the line went dead.

Skye turned to Cassidy, sobs billowing out from the depths of her and seizing her entire body.

"Cassidy, I feel like Serena has been thrown into the deep end of the water, and she has no idea how to swim, and I have no means of helping her. I can't stand this!"

Cassidy pulled her into a hug. "I know, sweetie. Don't worry. I'm not giving up. Not by a long shot."

"But—"

"Is everything okay?" The door opened, and Lisa stepped toward them. Even in the dark, Cassidy could hear the worry in her voice. "I thought I heard someone crying."

Skye sniffled and straightened, wiping her eyes with the sleeve of her shirt as she tried to quickly compose herself. "It's fine."

"You don't look fine." Lisa stepped closer, her eyes narrow with concern. "What's going on?"

"You should go back and enjoy your celebration," Skye said. "I didn't mean for you to see me like this."

"You're my friend. I want to help. Now would you please tell me what's going on?"

Cassidy and Skye exchanged a look. Finally Skye nodded her approval, giving Cassidy permission to share.

"Serena joined Gilead's Cove," Cassidy said softly.

Lisa gasped. "What? No . . ."

Skye nodded. "She did. And I can't get her back. She doesn't want out."

Lisa put her arm around Skye. "I can't believe this. I'm so sorry, sweetie."

"But this is your time, Lisa." Skye sucked in a shaky breath. "I don't want to ruin it. I want your big day to be perfect. I'm so sorry—"

"There's no such thing as perfect. Ever," Lisa said. "Besides, I can get married and still be there for you. The two aren't exclusive."

A sound behind them drew Cassidy's attention. She jerked her head toward the dark hallway leading to various Sunday school classrooms.

A footfall.

She'd heard a footfall.

But who would be walking through the utter blackness here? Especially without announcing himself?

Her spine tingled and her jaw clenched.

Had someone been there, listening to her and Skye this whole time?

Cassidy reached for the gun she still had holstered at her hip, her body going on alert.

"Guys," she whispered. "Do me a favor. Go back into the fellowship hall. Stay there. And tell Ty I need him."

Her friends froze, but only for a minute. They must have recognized the tone in her voice because they jumped into action, darting through the swinging doors.

As they did, Cassidy gripped her gun and turned toward the darkness.

She had to find out who was down the hallway.

Now.

She reached for the wall and flipped on the light switch just in time to see a man in black sprint toward the back door. As illumination hit him, she saw the gun holstered at his waist.

———

"CASSIDY SAID SHE NEEDS YOU." Skye's voice pulled Ty from his conversation with Braden as the two of them ate cake and chatted. "Now. In the hallway."

Ty left his plate on the table and quickly turned. Seeing the alarm on the faces around him, he tried to control his steps as he dashed toward the hallway. "Is she okay?"

"I think . . . I think she heard something." Skye's eyes were red-rimmed and her hands shook. "She didn't really leave any room for questions."

Just as Skye's voice trailed off, Ty heard someone in the distance yell, "Stop!"

Cassidy. That had been Cassidy.

Ty took off in a sprint. He pushed through the double doors into the hallway in time to see Cassidy disappear around the corner. Upping his speed, he took off after her.

As Ty burst through the back door and into the dark night, he nearly collided with his wife.

She put a finger over her lips, motioning for him to be quiet as she glanced around the parking lot.

He followed her gaze but saw nothing. No movement. Nothing suspicious.

Cautiously, Cassidy took the first step down the cement stairs at the back of the building. The parking lot, filled with probably thirty cars, surrounded them, offering easy hiding places for anyone who might try to conceal himself.

Just as their feet reached the gravel parking lot, noise erupted. A car roared to life and squealed away at breakneck speed.

"Come on!" Cassidy yelled.

Ty followed Cassidy to her police SUV. She cranked the engine and pulled out of the lot, trying to follow the car.

But it was too far in front of them, probably clocking one hundred miles an hour.

As the road curved half a mile ahead, the car disappeared from sight.

"You want to tell me what's going on?" Ty grabbed the bar above his head.

Cassidy seemed to grit her teeth before saying, "Someone was hiding in the hallway, listening to us."

"A bad guy?"

"If it was a good guy, why would he have a gun and run off?" Her grip looked white-knuckled on the steering wheel.

They rounded the bend, and an empty road stared back.

"What?" Cassidy muttered. "Where did he go?"

"There are a lot of roads here," Ty told her. "The driver could be on any one of them."

"Then I'll search each of them until I figure out where he went."

Cassidy made a hard-right turn onto a street and slowed as she cruised down it. There was no sign of the car or the person inside.

Three streets later, she hit the brakes and pointed at a driveway beneath a house. "There. That's the car."

She threw her SUV into Park and drew her gun.

"I've got your back," Ty said.

He pulled his gun from his waistband. He hardly ever left home without it. It was one of the effects of being a SEAL. He was always on guard.

Slowly, they moved side by side through the darkness.

There was no movement around them. No signs of life.

But that car was clearly parked beneath a house. Lights off. Not moving.

Cassidy reached the driver's side door and jerked it open.

Ty peered in behind her.

It was empty.

They glanced at each other.

That meant the driver was on foot. Or that he was hiding.

Still together, they searched the property. And the next property. And all the houses on the street and the next street over.

"He's gone," Ty said as they paused on some brittle grass between houses.

Cassidy frowned. "You're right. Maybe someone picked him up."

"Any idea who he was?"

"I have no clue." Cassidy's gaze met his. "But there's something I need to tell you, Ty. Something important."

Ty could see the tumultuous thoughts tossing inside her, and he braced himself for whatever she had to say.

CHAPTER NINE

TY LEANED BACK in his seat in the dark SUV and stared at the text message on Cassidy's phone. His stomach clenched so tightly that he felt himself jerk. "You got this message this morning, and you're just now telling me?"

Cassidy frowned, not bothering to start the car. She probably realized that with the way things were going, this might be their only moment of privacy, Ty mused. She could be right.

"I'm sorry." Her words sounded soft, gentle, as she shook her head and stared off into the darkness. "I should have mentioned it sooner."

"You should have."

"But we found those human remains, and then Serena disappeared, and . . . I don't know. Maybe I've been in denial." She swung her head back and forth, looking as if a heavy weight had been draped over her shoulders. "Besides, I knew if I told you that you'd want to drop everything to keep an eye on me."

"Of course, I would have."

Cassidy turned toward him, that same agony still present in her gaze as she studied him. "You have a life outside of me, Ty. You have to get things ready for your next session at Hope House. I don't want you to drop everything for this."

Ty considered bringing up his issues with Hope House, but now didn't seem to be the time. He had other more pressing points to drive home. "But you're my wife. You're always going to be my first priority. Always."

Cassidy skimmed her hand along his face and jaw, a sad smile tugging at the edge of her lips. "I love it that you're protective of me. I really do. But I can't live the rest of my life in fear or only thinking about the what ifs. This is my new reality. Forever."

"I understand that." Ty took her hand into both of his and planted a kiss on her knuckles.

He closed his eyes and let his lips linger there against her soft skin, battling thoughts of worst-case scenarios. He breathed in the clean scent of her skin and the faint aroma of her favorite vanilla-infused perfume.

"I found three hidden cameras at the house this morning," he admitted.

Cassidy tensed. "What?"

He told her about his discoveries.

"You have no idea where they came from or how they got there?" Cassidy asked.

"No idea. You know I like to keep an eye on things. We even have a security system in place. But someone was skilled enough to bypass it. I . . . I just don't know, Cassidy."

"I can send the cameras off to be tested. Maybe . . ."

Ty nodded. "It can't hurt."

"But you don't think it will tell us anything."

"I don't." Finally, in a raspy voice, Ty voiced his fears. "But what if DH-7 has found you?"

He couldn't bear the thought of it. He knew when he married Cassidy that their lives together would never be normal. But Ty had hoped for the best, hoped that the incident with DH-7 was behind them.

What if everything came to the surface again?

"What if this isn't DH-7?" Cassidy's voice cracked as she said the words.

Her question jolted him from his thoughts. "What do you mean?"

"I mean, there are other people who might want to harm me. This doesn't necessarily mean DH-7 has found me."

"Anthony Gilead?" Ty suggested, though he didn't find much comfort in that thought.

"Maybe. He likes control and power. Letting me know he knows my real identity would be one way to flex his muscles, so to speak."

Ty couldn't deny that the man was a manipulator

who liked to think he was the smartest man in the room but . . . "How would he have found out?"

"I don't know. I mean, the world thinks I'm dead. That a member of the gang shot and killed me. But that doesn't mean that if someone searched hard enough for information about me that they couldn't discover it."

Ty rubbed his jaw, liking this less and less. "Anthony Gilead seems like the type who does his homework."

"Yes, he does." Cassidy crossed her arms and stared out the window. "Anthony Gilead or DH-7 are the most likely culprits behind the text. But there are also those bodies that were discovered today. Someone didn't want us to find them and fired on me and my crew. Sometimes there are a few too many layers to the crime world here on this island."

"People see the secluded location and think it's perfect to accomplish their tasks." The unease in his gut grew as he said the words aloud.

"Just like the pirates of many years ago, I suppose."

"Exactly," Ty muttered.

Cassidy leaned toward him, her gaze softening. "Thanks for being in this with me."

"Always." As Ty reached for her, his hand slipped to her neck. Gently, he tugged her closer until their lips met. He didn't ever want to let her go.

No, sometimes Ty wanted to whisk Cassidy away from this place, take her somewhere she'd never be in danger again.

But life didn't work like that.

But he meant what he'd said. There was nothing he wouldn't do for Cassidy—nothing he wouldn't do to keep her safe.

He only wished that resolve wouldn't be tested again and again.

CASSIDY CALLED Skye and asked her to let Lisa know that she and Ty had to bow out of the rest of the wedding shower. Later, Cassidy would call Lisa herself to apologize. She hoped their disruption hadn't ruined things for the soon-to-be bride and groom.

But, as Cassidy stood on her screened-in porch with Kujo beside her, her thoughts remained on that figure who'd been hiding in the church's dark hallway.

She'd barely caught a glimpse of him, only enough to see that he was dressed in black and that he had a gun. She'd seen enough to know he was fast and nimble. Sensed enough to know he was dangerous.

But nothing else.

Cassidy had already run his plates and discovered that the car had been stolen from up in Hatteras last week. Could that person have been the traitor she feared was in her midst? Could it have been Dane or Leggott?

More anxiety squeezed at her gut.

She didn't know. And, until she did, she would have

to proceed with caution. She'd asked Dane to handle investigating the vehicle she'd chased, and then she'd headed home to attempt to rest.

As a breeze swept through the screen, she lifted her head, welcoming the cool wind and the scent of the sea that came with it. Something always comforted her about the earthy smell.

Her hands gripped the rough wood along the railing that lined the room. Tomorrow would be a new day, and, after some sleep, maybe Cassidy could think more clearly. More clearly about those bodies. About Serena. About the man hiding out at church during the wedding shower. About that text message.

That text message . . . every time she thought about it, Cassidy got chills. Who had sent it? Though she'd tried to remain composed for Ty, the thought of it shook Cassidy to the core.

If someone affiliated with DH-7 found her . . . she'd be a dead woman. There would be no greater accomplishment for the former gang members than to track down the supposed traitor who'd single-handedly torn apart the organization, and then kill her.

As Ty fixed them some popcorn, Cassidy remained where she was. Memories filled her. She didn't often think about Seattle and her old life. It had been two years since she'd gone deep undercover and left everything she'd ever known behind. It had been a year since she fled the trouble there and came here to this North Carolina island.

Lantern Beach was supposed to be only temporary. It had been a hiding place until she could go to trial, put the bad guys away, and then resume her old life.

Except, deep inside her, Cassidy knew she'd never resume her old life again.

Her dog, Colombo, now had a new home. Her parents, for the most part, had continued without her, managing their multi-million-dollar business. Though her dad had recently had a stroke, her parents seemed to be weathering the changes well. Their lives had always been separate from hers.

Then Cassidy had met Ty, and everything seemed to work out for the best. She preferred her life here to the life she'd had in Seattle. But maybe thinking that it would last forever was too good to be true.

Now the old could be threatening to catch up with the new.

The realization caused her head to pound.

Ty knocked on the window. "Popcorn is ready."

Cassidy waved to him and then stepped inside.

As she did, her phone rang. It was her friend Ernestine, the Lantern Beach newspaper editor. If Ernestine was calling at nine at night, then something was probably up. What now? How much more could Cassidy put on her plate without dropping everything?

"Hi, Ernestine," Cassidy answered.

"Cassidy, I just heard something that I thought you'd want to know."

"Please tell."

"I was talking to a friend who works down at the town office. She told me that someone else has entered the mayoral race. He got the paperwork in just in time, apparently."

"Okay. Who's that?" It didn't sound too serious—thank goodness.

"Cassidy . . . it's Anthony Gilead."

Cassidy's stomach clenched. Anthony Gilead? Running for mayor of Lantern Beach?

The whole idea was worse than horrible—it was abominable.

CHAPTER TEN

MORIAH AWOKE bright and early the next morning and got dressed. A surge of pride rushed through her as she rubbed the rose-scented lotion into her skin. Every time she smelled it, she felt powerful. Brave. Like she could conquer the world.

Moriah was going to be someone that others could look up to for wisdom. The progress she'd made since coming here felt amazing—exhilarating, for that matter.

Desperate not to fumble her latest task of being a mentor, Moriah had asked Serena to meet before breakfast. Moriah needed to teach her the way things were done here at the Cove. The girl seemed willing and enthusiastic to learn, and this could be Moriah's chance to prove to everyone here that she had what it took to do this. To be Gilead's bride and partner.

She stepped from her room and nearly collided with her fiancé.

Her chest filled with warmth when she saw Gilead, especially when a grin spread across his handsome face.

"Moriah, where are you going so bright and early?" He paused in front of her, his dark hair glistening, as if he'd just gotten out of the shower. Just recently, he'd begun growing a beard and mustache that he kept trimmed short. His figure wasn't necessarily buff, but he kept himself thin and healthy. To Moriah, he might as well be a movie star.

"I'm meeting my mentee." Pride stained her voice.

Something flickered through his gaze. "Is that right? Good. I'm sure you'll be great for her."

"I'll do my best." Moriah couldn't let Gilead down. She *wouldn't*.

He stepped closer. So close that his hands rested at her waist. That his head dipped toward hers. That his breath whispered across her cheek and caused a new round of tingles to invade her body.

"I need you to do one more thing for me," he said quietly.

"Of course. Anything." Moriah's voice sounded thin with anticipation. She always felt this way when Gilead was close. The man just did something to her.

"I need you to report back to me," he said.

Moriah had no idea what he was talking about, but she knew she'd do anything for him. "I'd be happy to report back to you."

He drew back enough to lock gazes with her and smiled before wrapping his arms around her. Moriah's head hit his chest as he pulled her close. Close enough that she could feel his heart beating against her own body. That she could hardly breathe.

Gilead kissed the top of her head and stroked her back, seeming to forget her wound was still healing. Every time he got close, she flinched, anticipating the pain.

"You trust me, don't you?" he whispered.

"Of course."

"Then relax." His hand veered dangerously close to her wound again.

"Of . . . of course," Moriah stumbled.

For a moment—just a flash, really—she felt trapped. Like she couldn't move. Couldn't get away.

Like Gilead was exercising some kind of power over her or something.

The thought was crazy . . . Gilead loved her. He just didn't realize how tightly he held her. Or how overwhelmed she felt.

"We shouldn't be this close yet," Gilead whispered. "I shouldn't be holding you like this. But I can hardly wait until our wedding, Moriah."

Her doubts scattered like seagulls being chased by a rowdy canine. "I feel the same."

"I have exciting things planned for us."

"Anything with you will be exciting." Moriah meant the words. Gilead was the most fascinating person she'd ever met.

His lips touched hers, and her emotions exploded inside her with so much force that she nearly felt dizzy.

As quickly as the kiss started, it ended. But Gilead didn't move. He remained near the wall, studying Moriah's face with . . . some kind of glimmer in his gaze.

As her dizziness receded, she remembered Gilead's earlier words. *I need you to do something for me. I need you to report back.*

"You didn't tell me what I needed to report to you," Moriah said.

His hands, at one time tugging on her back, now burrowed into her skin with enough force that Moriah flinched. Gilead must not realize that he was hurting her. Otherwise, he would stop.

In the distance, the sounds of breakfast being prepared—the clanging of pots and pans—echoed up the stairway. The subtle scent of food—maybe eggs or it could even be oatmeal, Moriah wasn't sure—drifted up also, making her stomach rumble.

"I need you to talk to your new mentee and find out any information you can on Cassidy Chambers."

The breath left her lungs as Ruth's words echoed back to her. *I've seen the way Gilead looks at that woman, the police chief. There's more there than a professional curiosity.*

What if Ruth was right? What if Gilead—her Gilead—actually was in love with Cassidy? Could a man desire two women? Could God direct a man to have more than one wife?

Moriah didn't know. But all the certainty she'd felt just moments ago about Ruth being wrong vanished like the fog on a sunny day.

"Did you hear me?" Gilead's fingers pressed deeper until Moriah let out a groan.

"Yes, I heard you. But why—"

"It's not your job to question me. I just need you to do as I ask. Do you understand?" His voice took on a hard edge.

Moriah had angered him. Her questions were pestering. Her best friend growing up had always told Moriah that—told her that she needed to let things go.

Shame filled her.

Gilead hardly ever got mad. Yet Moriah had managed to bring it out in him. She'd thought she was maturing, but maybe she was wrong. Maybe she was the same old worthless Moriah Roberts she'd always been.

"Yes, I understand," she finally said, but her voice sounded breathless.

A smile tugged at Gilead's face again, and he released his grip on her. "Good. That's what I was hoping you'd say. Try to get any information you can from her."

"Yes, Gilead."

"Make her like you," he coached. "Then she'll do

whatever you want. You just have to know how to handle people."

"I'll do my best."

"Good girl. We're going to be so happy together, you know that?" Gilead stepped back.

As he did, the tightness in Moriah's lungs eased, and she drew in a deep breath. "Yes, we will be."

He lowered his head until his lips barely touched her neck. "Only two more days."

A shiver raked through Moriah, but she didn't know why. A shiver of excitement? Of fear?

It was just anxiety, she realized. Marriage was a big step. Especially marriage to a powerful man like Anthony Gilead.

And, though part of her wanted to question him why he wanted information on Police Chief Cassidy Chambers, Moriah knew better. Maybe once they were married it would be different. He would be more open. He'd listen to her more.

Right now, Gilead was just as distracted as she was.

But soon everything would be better. All Moriah had to do was say, "I do."

Then her life was going to change.

CHAPTER ELEVEN

BEFORE CASSIDY WENT into the office the next morning, she headed down to the ferry docks. She knew it was a longshot, but she wanted to speak with the superintendent there. Maybe—just maybe—in all of his treks from Lantern Beach to Ocracoke, he'd seen something suspicious going on at the lighthouse beach.

She parked and sauntered toward the office area. A man in a khaki uniform stopped her before she reached the door. "Can I help you?"

Cassidy stared up at the man, whose intense eyes bore into hers like a bodyguard on duty. "I need to talk to Superintendent Rodgers."

"Your name?"

"Chief Chambers." Cassidy had thought she'd met most of the people on the island at this point. But not everyone who worked the ferry system lived on the island.

"One minute."

As he walked inside the building, Cassidy paced over to the drink machines. Against her better instincts, she put three quarters into one of the slots and was rewarded with a dewy, cold can of Coke. She tried not to drink too many, but sometimes the extra caffeine and sugar were just what she needed.

As she waited, she spotted a collection bin for stuffed animals. The laminated sign taped to the front advertised that the donations would go to children in need in the Outer Banks.

She hadn't realized that donations were allowed here at the docks, but the gesture was nice.

"Can I help you?"

Cassidy turned and offered a smile to Rodgers. The man seemed friendly enough, though the northeast native could be brisk at times, which turned some locals off.

"Good morning," she called.

"Oh, it's you, Cassidy." His shoulders relaxed. "Sorry. I'm fielding calls about having the ferry system shut down last week. You wouldn't believe how many people are still angry about that, and I don't have time to deal with everyone personally."

"I guess it cut some time out of people's vacations since they couldn't get to the island, not to mention the fishing tournament." Cassidy popped the top of her drink and took a quick sip.

"And now they want us to reimburse them. That's

why I have one of my guys acting as secretary. None of us have enjoyed the hate mail we've been getting about that."

"I can imagine."

He straightened. "Now, what can I do for you?"

"Listen, we're investigating a case right now, and I'm wondering if you may have inadvertently seen anything while en route. It's the area by the lighthouse beach. Have you noticed anything going on there?"

"Heard about the dead bodies."

"Did you?" Nothing stayed quiet for long on this island.

"Wayne Waters and I play poker together. He swore me to secrecy."

"And everyone else who was there as well, I assume."

Rodgers shrugged. "Of course. Anyway, I've been thinking about that beach ever since I heard about those bodies. I have to say that I haven't seen anything taking place there, though. Occasionally, I'll see a fishing buddy out there. But no one else."

Cassidy bit her lip, disappointed that he didn't know anything more. She nodded anyway and thanked him. "If you think of anything, let me know. In the meantime, maybe I'll get some donations for your stuffed animal drive here. Nice touch since everyone is so mad at you right now."

Rodgers smiled. "Whatever we can do to make the community better. Have a good day, Cassidy."

"You too."

———

AFTER LEAVING THE DOCKS, Cassidy went to her office and made a list of everything she needed to do. If she didn't write it down, she knew it would never get marked off. No, her thoughts were going in too many different directions.

First, she needed to track the cell phone number connected to that threatening text she'd gotten about her past. She knew that most likely it was a burner phone and the information would lead nowhere. But she had to at least try.

She also needed to follow up with Abbott about the human remains found on the beach, see if there were any updates.

She needed to touch base with Dane about the stolen vehicle from last night.

She needed to do some more research on Anthony Gilead's run for mayor.

She needed to look for any loopholes that would get Serena out of Gilead's Cove.

Cassidy rubbed her temples. The tasks felt overwhelming, but she just needed to start at the top and see what she could discover.

She took a long sip of coffee before picking up her phone and putting in a call about that cell phone number. The fact that Cassidy was digging into this had to be a secret. She didn't want anyone asking questions or she might have to explain about that text.

Ten minutes later, Cassidy confirmed what she already knew—the text had come from a burner phone, and the device was now inactive and untraceable.

Not surprising.

Next, Cassidy called Abbott, who didn't answer. She left a message for him to call her back about the dead bodies they'd discovered. Most likely, the NCSBI hadn't learned anything of value yet, but Cassidy wanted to know for sure.

Deciding to stretch her legs, she went into Dane's office to get an update from him. Ranger, a boxer mix, lay beside the desk near him and wagged his tail when Cassidy walked in.

"Oh, hey, Chief." Dane looked up from his paperwork. "What's going on?"

"I need to follow up with you about that stolen vehicle from last night." She knelt and rubbed Ranger's head.

Dane put his papers down. "Oh, right. I had it towed here to the station for impound. I ran the plates and discovered the Honda was stolen from Hatteras last week. The owner—a man from Michigan—was on a fishing trip. He came back to the parking lot at the inlet to discover his vehicle was gone. He's anxious to get it back as soon as it's cleared."

"Any evidence inside?" Cassidy took another sip of her coffee.

Dane shook his head. "No, nothing. There were no food wrappers, cans, bottles. I didn't even find any mud, sand, or hair. I swept the entire car."

"Fingerprints?" She knew it was a longshot, but she had to ask.

"No, everything was wiped clean. Was your guy last night wearing gloves?"

Cassidy shrugged and tried to picture their chase. Everything had happened so quickly, and it had been dark outside. "I don't know. I couldn't see him that well. He was wearing black clothing. He very well could have had black gloves on as well."

"He certainly seemed to cover his bases." Dane paused and studied Cassidy for a moment, as if trying to put the pieces together. "You think this has something to do with those human remains?"

"I have no idea. Considering someone shot at us on-scene yesterday, I'd say it's a good possibility." Then again, it could be a member of DH-7. Cassidy kept that thought to herself.

"Any updates on those human remains?" Dane asked.

As if on cue, Cassidy's phone rang. She glanced at the screen and saw that it was Abbott. She hoped he might have some news for her.

CHAPTER TWELVE

CASSIDY EXCUSED herself and put her phone to her ear. "Abbott, thanks for the call back."

"I assume you're calling to check in about the case." His voice sounded dour, as if he resented her earlier interruption.

She didn't care. "Yes, I was."

"We haven't been able to discover much yet. These things take time."

Though Cassidy wasn't surprised, disappointment still bit at her. "I figured as much."

"However," Abbott continued. "There is one victim who might be easier to identify. We're guessing her age to be about twenty-five. She had traces of long red hair. And, because of a medical condition, we think we may be able to trace her more easily."

Cassidy closed her door, anxious to hear more. "What's the medical condition?"

"Scoliosis."

A curvature of the spine . . . interesting. "Well, that should certainly narrow things down."

"That's what we're hoping." He paused. "Any news on your end?"

After sitting in her chair, Cassidy told him about the chase last night at Lisa and Braden's wedding shower. "I'll let you know if I hear anything."

"Thanks, Chief. Oh, and there is one more thing I thought I should mention to you."

"What's that?" Cassidy leaned back, hoping his news was something of value. She could use some good news.

"As I'm sure you remember, several weeks ago, you and I talked about looking into Anthony Gilead after he claimed to have legally changed his name."

"Right, but we had to go state by state to find record of it, and, so far, we haven't had any luck." She sighed. The man almost seemed like a ghost sometimes.

"Exactly. I thought I'd let you know that we got a hit."

Cassidy's pulse spiked. "Please share."

"It was from down in Florida. It turns out that Anthony Gilead's real name is Gerrard Becker. He legally changed it three years ago."

"Is that all you know?"

"So far. We just got the report back this morning, so I haven't had time to look into it any further. But I knew you'd want to know right away."

"Thanks for sharing," Cassidy said. "On that note, maybe I should let you know that Anthony Gilead—aka Gerrard Becker—just completed all the paperwork, and he's now officially running for mayor."

"Mayor of Lantern Beach?" Abbott sounded just as surprised as Cassidy felt.

"That's the one."

"That's . . . disturbing, to say the least. I'd hate to see what that man would do if he was in power. Your job will become ten times harder, for sure, if he's your boss."

"Don't remind me."

Abbott let out a soft, thoughtful grunt before asking, "Any ideas on how to stop him?"

"I'm about to look into the legalities of his run. Gilead, of course, has to be a resident for at least ninety days. He's a smart man, so I'm pretty sure he's covered all his bases. But one can hope . . ."

"If it makes you feel better, I'm sure no one will vote for him."

Cassidy wanted to believe the same. But she'd seen the impossible happen before. And that was the last thing she wanted to see happen here on Lantern Beach.

———

THREE HOURS LATER, Cassidy took a sip from her water bottle and stared at the computer screen. Gerrard Becker. Thirty-three years old. Originally from a small town in Delaware. His dad had worked for the railroad. His mom had been an RN.

Gerrard had gone to college to study theology and had pastored a small congregation for two years after graduation. But there were four years missing from his timeline. There was no job record. No social media presence. No financial information.

Nothing.

So where had the man gone for four years? Had Gerrard been in the Middle East, looking for the ancient book of Makir like he claimed? If so, why were there no articles published on his so-called accomplishment? And why had he changed his name? People didn't do that for no reason.

Cassidy leaned back in her chair, thinking things through and trying to figure out if she could in some way leverage this information to help see Serena in person.

Maybe Cassidy could call Gilead's mom or dad. Some old college co-eds. See what she could learn about the man.

The more she knew, the more knowledge Cassidy would be armed with when she went into battle.

The phone rang. It was Abbott again. At least he was staying true to his word and keeping her in the loop.

"Hey, Abbott," she answered.

"I think we have a hit on one of the victims."

Cassidy sat up, curiosity pulsing through her. "What did you find out?"

"There's someone in a missing person's report who matches the description of our victim with scoliosis. She disappeared about six months ago, so the timeline adds up."

"Tell me more."

"Her name was Reagan Craven. She was twenty-eight, and she grew up in eastern Kentucky."

Eastern Kentucky . . . that could potentially be a connection with Gilead. His hunting ground when starting the cult had been in the West Virginia area, and the two states backed up to each other.

"Did you talk to her family?" Cassidy asked.

"As a matter of fact, yes. I talked to her father. Reagan was an only child. She left home and said she needed a new start. She and her father weren't particularly close, so he didn't keep tabs on her. But she'd mentioned starting over at the beach. It had always been her favorite place."

"So you're thinking she came here to Lantern Beach to get her fresh start? Certainly someone would have noticed her if she'd become a permanent resident."

"You would think. Or she could have blended in with the tourists and become a hermit during the cooler months."

"Maybe. But that still doesn't explain how she died."

"No, it doesn't. But she wasn't sick. Of course, we're

still testing the bones and DNA to figure out how these people died. But you might want to consider there could be a serial killer on the loose."

"A serial killer? I think that's a bit extreme."

"Three bodies, Chief."

A chill washed over her, but Cassidy shoved her emotions aside. "So, will you keep digging? See if you can find some of her friends?"

"Of course. I just wanted to give you that update in case it triggered anything."

"It's not my case, but do you mind if I talk to some people around here and see if anyone recognizes her?"

"No, I'd appreciate the help. I'll send her photo."

"Sounds good."

As Cassidy hung up, another text message came in. This one was from Mac.

Gilead doing rally down at boardwalk.

What? The man was trying to win over the locals as well?

Cassidy slipped on her jacket and called Ty.

She wanted to go see this for herself.

But, even more than that, she wanted to figure out a way to put an end to the craziness before it got even more out of control.

CHAPTER THIRTEEN

TY STOOD with Mac and Wes and listened as Anthony Gilead spoke from behind a small podium on a portable stage.

The ocean crashed behind the man, creating a picturesque scene perfect for magazine covers or social media. Even the sun seemed to cooperate as it shone down from above like a spotlight that both drew attention and offered a touch of warmth to anyone who gathered.

Just what Gilead had been hoping for, Ty had to assume.

The man wore a dark suit with a blue tie and smiled, showing his pearly whites. He was a master manipulator. And now he was trying to use his charm to become mayor.

Why? Why would he do this?

Power, Ty decided. This was all about power.

And a man who wanted to be in power that badly was the last person who *should* be in power. That was Ty's experience, at least.

"I've got to say, the man has a good stage presence," Wes whispered beside him. Wes, one of Ty's closest friends, was a part-time plumber, part-time kayak guide, and certified bachelor.

"He's a classic narcissist." Mac scowled at the stage.

"You're not feeling threatened, are you?" Wes ribbed Mac.

Mac's scowl only deepened. "Threatened? By him? No. I've got different tactics. Old-fashioned ones. I'm going door-to-door to talk to residents."

Someone sidled up beside him. Ty looked over and spotted Cassidy. She squeezed his arm, but her gaze was fixated on the stage.

"He's actually got a crowd?" she muttered. "Are these all folks from Gilead's Cove?"

"We couldn't be that lucky," Ty said. "These are mostly locals, with a few vacationers thrown in."

"How did he put this together so quickly?" Cassidy's eyes crinkled at the edges, as if she were perplexed. "You have to have permits for this stuff."

"It doesn't take long to be approved down at the town administration office," Mac said. "Gilead probably got the permit last night after his application was filed and approved. He could have received word this morning and set this up."

They grew silent as Gilead's words became louder, more adamant.

"I believe that Lantern Beach is a great place and that, under the right leadership, it can be even greater," Gilead said as people around him cheered. "I believe we should keep the old-fashioned charm of this area. We need to stay small—that's why people come here. Because Lantern Beach is different. Because it's warm— and I'm not talking about the temperature in the summer. I'm talking about people's hospitality."

More cheers.

Ty could hardly stand to watch it.

"We know his real name," Cassidy leaned closer and muttered. "It's Gerrard Becker. He's from Delaware."

Ty's pulse spiked, and he gladly turned his attention away from this mockery of a speech being given. "Anything else?"

"I just got the information before you called, so I still have to dig deeper. But there is a strange absence in his timeline of about four years. There's nothing on him during that period."

Could that be because Gilead was in the Middle East? Ty thought it could be a possibility. Something about the man seemed familiar, but the memories felt buried and unreachable.

"How long ago?" Ty whispered.

"Six years ago is when he disappeared from everyone's radar," Cassidy said. "He jumped back onto the scene as Anthony Gilead two years ago, and it's led to this."

Six years ago? That's when Ty had been a SEAL. When he'd been in the Middle East. When he'd performed that rescue that had changed his life.

He still thought Gilead had some kind of connection to the ordeal, but he just couldn't figure out what.

They all went quiet for a moment and listened to Gilead again.

"I believe Lantern Beach is the greatest place in the world and that it's filled with the greatest people in the world." Gilead flashed his million-dollar smile, his teeth gleaming in the sunlight. "But everything can be made better. The cost of living here has skyrocketed. I know that you've been taxed too much for too long, and I want to change that."

A cheer rose from the crowd.

Ty's eyebrows flickered up. These people were buying what Gilead had to say. What were they think-ing? Couldn't they see through him?

"Money isn't everything, but with money comes freedom. Freedom to do what you want. To live how you want. To make yourself a better person. To make the community a better place. That's why I believe we need to see more of our money in our own pockets."

Another cheer.

Mac grunted beside Ty.

"Certainly people know it's not as easy as he makes it sound," Mac said. "These are great promises that are hard to deliver on. He obviously has no idea how the system works. Next thing you know, he's going to want to ban cars on the island and make everyone ride bicycles and get solar panels. We can be a self-sustaining island, just like his little Gilead's Cove is trying to be."

Just then, Gilead's gaze fell on Ty, and the man's smile changed from a plastic politician to someone with an underlying agenda—one that was directed at Ty.

Where do I know you from? Ty mused. *Where?*

That question would continue to haunt Ty until he had some answers.

———

AFTER THE GUYS left to help Lisa move some tables for the wedding reception, Cassidy remained at the boardwalk. She watched as the crowd began to clear after Gilead's rally. She looked at each of the people present.

Laney Fredrickson? Bill Williams? Jack Melvin?

Why in the world had these locals come out to support this man? How had they even heard about the rally with such short notice? Cassidy suspected that Gilead had been planning this for longer than it appeared.

A few people stuck around to talk to Gilead, but Cassidy's attention remained on the two men on either side of Gilead.

She'd seen one man with him before. She thought his name was Enoch. The other she didn't recognize.

But they were almost acting as bodyguards for the man. Did he see himself as a superstar? Most likely, yes.

Cassidy waited until everyone else had cleared before approaching Gilead. He seemed to try and disarm her with his bright smile, but charm had never worked on Cassidy.

"I'm so glad you could make it," Gilead started, shoving his hands deep into his pockets and leaning back casually. "It's always nice to see your beautiful face."

"I wasn't here to support you." Cassidy's jaw clenched as she said the words. How could the man be so glib right now?

His smile remained unfazed. "Well, a man can dream, right?"

Cassidy stepped closer and lowered her voice. "Why are you doing this, Gilead? Why are you running for office? What do you want to prove?"

"So many questions." His tone sounded mocking.

Cassidy crossed her arms, waiting for a real answer.

Gilead tugged at his sleeves and smiled at someone who walked past, transforming into a showman type of politician before reverting back to the sleazy cult leader Cassidy knew he was.

"I want to make the island better, of course." Gilead's gaze fell on Cassidy again. "I've always been interested in politics."

Cassidy didn't buy it. "Why here?"

"I meant my earlier words. Lantern Beach is a slice

of heaven. Why *not* Lantern Beach? That would be the better question."

"It was one thing when you set up your little community here on the island. We're not going to let you take over this entire town, though. I already know you've been buying up properties whenever you have the chance. No doubt, you're using the money of the people who follow you."

His eyebrows flickered up. "It's always tricky for police chiefs to espouse their political views. I'd hate for the current mayor to find out about that, if you did. I heard he's looking for a reason to fire you."

Her spine tightened. "How would you have heard that?"

Gilead's satisfied smile said it all. "I'm very observant, Chief. What can I say?"

He did have a spy, didn't he? Someone in her circle.

But who? Who could it possibly be?

Cassidy didn't know. But she wouldn't have a moment of peace until she did.

CHAPTER FOURTEEN

CASSIDY STEPPED CLOSER to the man who was quickly becoming her nemesis, anger burning through her veins. "I don't know what your end game is here, Gilead—or should I say Gerrard Becker? But I will figure it out. I'll stop it."

His smile slipped. "You discovered my other name."

Now it was Cassidy's turn to feel the strangely comforting surge of satisfaction. "I did. And I can't wait to discover more about you."

"I think you should stay out of my past, Chief." Gilead's voice darkened, though his demeanor remained cheery—clearly a façade for anyone watching.

"Why is that?"

"People shouldn't go poking around into other people's pasts. Wouldn't you agree?"

Was Gilead hinting that he knew about Cassidy's

past? Was he the one who'd sent her that text? Without admitting too much, Cassidy couldn't ask him.

And that was probably just what the man wanted—to feel that flash of satisfaction in knowing Cassidy couldn't even confront him about it.

"I'd love to stay and chat longer, but I must go." Gilead turned to his two cronies on either side of him. "I've got a campaign to plan."

Cassidy edged herself in front of him, not yet done with this conversation. "If you do one thing to hurt Serena Lavinia, I will find you and personally see to it that you pay."

Gilead tilted his head, almost looking as if he enjoyed her words. "Is that a threat?"

"I mean it, Gilead," Cassidy continued. "You better not lay a finger on her."

"We're a peaceful group, Chief. How many times do I have to say that? Just because Barnabas made some poor choices, that doesn't mean we're all like that."

Barnabas had been a member of Gilead's Cove and was one of the first people from the compound Cassidy had met. The man—his real name was Gary Largo—had encouraged another man to commit suicide.

Barnabas later took his own life in a fire to avoid the consequences of what he'd done. Or maybe he'd laid down his life in order to avoid giving up information on the group that he'd transformed his life for.

Cassidy would never know.

"If you were peaceful, you wouldn't keep your people trapped behind those gates." Cassidy stared at Gilead, waiting for his rebuke.

He glanced around, as if making sure no one else had heard her, and then he chuckled, deflecting her statement and making Cassidy seem like the off-balanced one. "People can come and go as they please, Cassidy. No one is chained to the community. We just believe it's a safe place. Some people are meant for safe places, while others are meant to go and sow seeds outside."

"Your scouts, you mean?"

Surprise flashed in Gilead's gaze before quickly disappearing. "Yes, my scouts. We have the truth, Cassidy. Of course, we want to share it and see our numbers grow. You probably believe the same about your faith."

"Your faith and mine are nothing alike."

He leaned closer. "I wouldn't be so sure."

With that, he walked away.

Cassidy fisted her hands at her sides, wishing more than anything she could drive that man off this island.

———

"HE ACTUALLY SAID THAT?" Ty repeated. "Gilead told you to stay out of his past?"

Cassidy nodded as she grabbed another french fry

and dipped it into some special sauce Lisa had put together. "That's right."

Lisa had invited everyone over for lunch. The gang tried to get together at least once a week. After helping Lisa transform the Crazy Chefette restaurant into a reception hall, everyone had been famished.

"That means Anthony Gilead is hiding something." Mac sat back in the booth and nodded confidently.

Cassidy grabbed another fry. They were especially crisp today and offered just the comfort Cassidy sought —unfortunately. "I agree. And he's a master at it. This man knows exactly what he's doing. He's a born manipulator."

"Did he say anything about Serena?" Skye asked, her gaze still fraught with worry. She hadn't even touched her food, but her straw had been twisted until it was unrecognizable.

"I asked him, and he only said what Dietrich had already said." Cassidy wished she had better news. "That Serena came by her own free will and that she can leave of her own free will."

As Skye frowned, Austin put his arm around her. "I just wish I could talk to her. That I could see her face-to-face."

"I'm still working on it," Cassidy promised.

Skye's apologetic gaze met Cassidy's. "I know you are, Cassidy. I don't mean to put so much pressure on you. I just can't stop thinking about her, though."

Cassidy reached across the table and squeezed her friend's hand. "If Serena was my niece, I'd be worried too. Don't apologize."

A moment of silence fell, and everyone munched on their savory crab and jalapeno soup, grilled gouda sandwiches, and fries. Cassidy glanced around at the people she was closest to here on the island. Lisa and Braden, Skye and Austin, Wes, Mac . . .

What if it was someone in her circle of friends who was betraying her?

She mentally shook her head. No, no one here would do that.

Then again, who would?

Cassidy didn't want to face the fact that it could be someone she trusted. But the evidence was pointing more and more in that direction.

Wes finally cleared his throat, breaking up the quiet that captured the group.

"So what are you going to do to step up your political game, Mac?" Wes turned to the former police chief.

Mac shrugged and pushed away his empty plate. "Nothing. I'm going to keep doing what I'm doing. People around here know me and trust me."

"It's more important now than ever that you win, though." Lisa paused by the table, her white apron splattered with the creative juices from one of her newest creations. "We can't let Gilead be elected."

"And no one wants Tomlinson to stay in office,"

Austin said. "He's a joke. He's done nothing to earn the position. He just happens to be from the right family."

"Not to mention he's a jerk," Ty added.

"If I were a drinking man, I'd offer a toast for that one." Wes frowned and rolled his eyes.

"We could have a party for you here at my place, Mac," Lisa said. "You know, a meet and greet."

"I think you have enough planning on your hands." Mac tilted his head and cast her a fatherly look. "You're getting married in two days."

"I know, but everything is planned and ready. I just have to be there at this point."

Lisa was the calmest bride Cassidy had ever seen.

"It's one of the perks of not having a big, fancy wedding," Lisa continued. "There's less stress and more time to enjoy the journey."

"I really don't want to put you out," Mac continued.

"You're not," Lisa told him. "It will be nice to have something to make the time pass more quickly until my big day. How about tomorrow afternoon?"

Mac lowered his glass of water. "Are you sure you can throw something together that soon?"

"I'm sure," Lisa said. "It will be fun."

"I'll help her." Skye's gaze perked for a moment. "I need to keep my mind occupied."

"We can all pitch in," Austin added. "That's what friends are for, right?"

"And for entertainment, Clemson can bring his educational skeleton in and dance with it," Wes added.

"Don't tell me I'm the only one who's seen him doing that?"

A smile tugged at Cassidy's lips. She loved these people. She really did.

But how could she possibly keep them all safe?

She had no idea.

CHAPTER FIFTEEN

AFTER LUNCH, Cassidy went back to work. Lisa had sent her away with some salt and vinegar potato chip cookies—another one of her specialties. Though Cassidy had balked initially at the idea, the treats had become one of her favorites, and she knew she'd be nibbling on them for the rest of the day.

As soon as she was behind her desk, Cassidy picked up her phone to call Kaleb Walker's number. She knew it was a long shot, but she decided to reach out to him anyway.

Kaleb was an attorney as well as a member of Gilead's Cove who lived out here in the community. Cassidy had helped him find his sister, Lela, just over a week ago. But, after that, the man had disappeared back into the mysterious folds of the cult. Was he too afraid to leave? Or did he really love it so much that he'd give up everything and everyone to stay?

Cassidy had no idea.

But after helping him out earlier, Cassidy had planned on calling in a favor from him. She figured this was as good a time as ever. She wanted to know if Reagan Craven had any connection to the group and find out what he knew about Serena being there.

Had Reagan simply been an innocent tourist here on the island, someone who'd wandered into the wrong place at the wrong time?

Maybe.

Cassidy broke off a piece of cookie and popped it into her mouth, still mulling things over.

Unlike Abbott, Cassidy didn't believe they had a serial killer here on the island. She wasn't sure how those people had died, but she intended to find out.

She dialed Kaleb's number and listened as he answered on the second ring.

"Why are you calling me, Chief?" he whispered.

"I need your help."

"You can't call me like this. I'm not even supposed to have this phone. I thought I told you that."

"What will Gilead do to you if he sees you with it?" The question was baited, and Cassidy knew it. She waited to hear what he'd say.

Kaleb didn't respond for a moment, as if gathering his thoughts. "It's not like that. But I'm breaking the rules. I could be kicked out."

"That might be the best thing that ever happened to you. Ask Lela."

"Don't bring my sister into this." Anger edged into his voice, and Cassidy knew she'd hit a nerve.

She wasn't ready to let this drop yet, though. "I believe Gilead threatened that if Lela didn't stay quiet, he would harm you. How does that make you feel?"

"He wouldn't do something like that."

"I think he would. But that's not why I called." As much as Cassidy would love to convince him to abandon ship at the Cove, she had other matters to discuss.

"You have ten seconds."

Cassidy leaned back in her seat and stared at the picture of Reagan Craven Abbott sent her. "I need to know if a woman was affiliated with Gilead's Cove."

"I'm not your personal assistant or something. I prefer not to be in the middle of your investigations."

"I'd prefer Gilead's Cove not be on Lantern Beach. But since that's not a possibility, I've got to make the best of this."

"Who is she?" Kaleb asked after a moment of silence.

Cassidy stared at the redhead on her screen. "Her name is Reagan Craven."

"Doesn't ring any bells," he answered quickly.

He wasn't getting out of it this easily. "I'll text you her picture, just in case she used a different name."

"I doubt she's someone I know." Kaleb sounded irritated and rushed.

"If she is, I need to know. Understand?"

He hesitated again. "I understand."

"Great. I'm sending it as soon as I end this call."

He sighed but didn't argue.

She had one more question for him. "And have you seen Serena Lavinia there at the compound?"

"Who?"

"She's a friend of Dietrich's."

Kaleb grunted. "I can't keep tabs on everyone who comes through here. Now, I've got to go."

The line went dead.

True to her word, Cassidy sent the picture and then waited. A few minutes later, Kaleb replied with:

Don't know her.

Cassidy frowned and replied:

That's not what I asked. Have you seen her?

She waited but got no response. After several minutes, she called him. He didn't answer.

She clenched her jaw.

What did Kaleb know? Why had Reagan come to this island? And what exactly had happened to her after she arrived?

Someone knocked at her door. Cassidy looked up and saw Melva, the PD receptionist and dispatcher, standing there with the same anxious expression on her face that she always wore. The woman, who was in her late fifties, always had a grandmotherly vibe, with her short, poofy hair and matronly looking clothes.

"Chief, we just got a phone call from the town

administration," she started. "Bob Anderson didn't come into work today."

Bob Anderson was the town clerk and a hard worker. "How does that involve us?"

"Apparently, his secretary has tried calling him and even went to his home. He's not answering. She said this is very unlike him, and she wants to know if someone can go check on him."

"Call her back and tell her I'm going out there myself."

"Yes, Chief."

Cassidy knew it probably wasn't anything. But maybe some fresh air would help her clear her head.

———

CASSIDY BROUGHT Dane with her to Bob's place. His home was more unique than most of the houses in the area. Shaped like an octagon with a rounded roof, it had been painted bright purple. Cassidy didn't know the story behind his house, but everyone in the island knew where it was.

Turn at the corner by Bob Anderson's house.

Go past Bob Anderson's purple house two blocks, and you're there.

If you reach Bob Anderson's house, you've gone too far.

Cassidy supposed there were good things about having such a unique residence.

The strange thing was that the place didn't seem to fit Bob at all. She'd met the man several times, and he was quiet and demure. From what she remembered, Bob was single and in his mid-fifties. He'd always seemed nice enough.

She parked on the gravel space near his stairway and climbed to the front door.

"These calls are always my favorite," Dane said.

"Why's that?"

"Half the time, I find the person we're looking for either passed out drunk or caught in a compromising position, if you know what I mean."

Cassidy nodded. "Yeah, I've had that happen a couple times."

"Here in Lantern Beach?" Dane asked.

"No, in—" She almost said Seattle. She bit her tongue and quickly remembered her cover. "Back in Texas when I worked there."

"That's right. Funny, though, you don't remind me of a Texas gal."

"And how are Texas gals supposed to seem?" Cassidy kept her voice light.

He shrugged. "I don't know. I suppose I expect more of a twang. Of course, you've got the sass and confidence I should expect."

"Well, Texas is a big state." Was Dane fishing for information or just making chitchat? Cassidy wasn't sure, but it was best to move on from this conversation.

She pounded on Bob's door and waited.

Just as she suspected, there was no answer. The deck, however, stretched around the perimeter of the house.

"You go left, I'll go right," Cassidy said.

"Ten-four."

She breathed easier as soon as Dane was out of sight. Cassidy had almost said Seattle. She thought she was more careful than that. But she'd been thinking about home too much lately, especially after she'd received that threatening text.

She needed to be more careful in the future, though. Letting her guard down was always a bad, bad idea.

Cassidy peered in the first window and saw an empty living room. Nothing seemed strange or out of place. However, she had noted that there was a car parked beneath the house. That alone indicated that Bob was most likely home.

The next window showed much of the same, just from a slightly different angle. Still nothing.

She suspected it would be the same for the next two windows. They all lined a great room that appeared empty.

"Chief, come see this!" Dane called from the other side of the house.

She quickly glanced through the other windows as she went past and met Dane.

"Does that look like a shoe to you?" He nodded toward the window beside him.

Cassidy peered inside, cupping her eyes against the

glare. She sucked in a breath. That most certainly did look like a shoe. One that was attached to a leg, attached to a body behind the bed.

"Call the paramedics. And then we need to get inside."

CHAPTER SIXTEEN

"WHAT DO YOU THINK?" Cassidy asked Doc Clemson after he'd arrived at the scene and done a preliminary examination of Bob Anderson.

Bob had been found on the floor beside his bed. He was dressed, as if he'd planned to go to work. His toothbrush was even wet, as if he'd brushed his teeth. Cassidy had checked.

There were no signs that anything physical had happened—no blood or broken bones. The décor in his house—minimalist and simple—remained untouched, and everything was in its place. There were no signs of a break-in.

"It's hard to say without an autopsy," Clemson said. "But I do know that Bob had some heart problems. It wouldn't surprise me if his ticker stopped ticking, to put it lightly."

"I'm sorry to hear that."

"Me too. Bob was a nice guy."

"If you say so," Cassidy agreed, even though she knew good and well that nice was subjective, and even nice guys could have their secrets. "By the way, I know this seems off subject, but, as town clerk, was Bob in charge of elections around here?"

Clemson stood and raised his eyebrows. "As a matter of fact, I believe he was. Why would you ask that?"

Cassidy shrugged. "Just wondering."

His eyebrows crept even higher. "I highly doubt that."

Cassidy crossed her arms and stared down at the dead man, trying to picture the last moments of his life. "I think the timing is strange. I mean, Anthony Gilead gets in at the last minute and is on the ballot for mayor. The next day, the man who approved it is found dead."

"You think Gilead could be involved with this?" Clemson frowned down at Bob.

"I didn't necessarily say that," Cassidy said. "I just think the timing is strange."

"Maybe the autopsy will tell us more."

"That's what I'm hoping." She shifted. "I also think it's strange that our victims who were left in the woods had no signs of any physical trauma."

"You think this is connected?"

"I don't think anything yet. I just want to be open-minded and explore every possibility. Four dead bodies in a week? I'd be a fool to not question if they were linked."

"We should know something soon," Clemson said. "The evidence will tell, right?"

"The evidence will tell. In the meantime, I'll talk to people at his office and make sure he wasn't having any conflicts we need to know about."

Cassidy knew this new theory could be nothing. It could be a coincidence. But it also could be something—something big. But she needed confirmation before she ran away with that new theory.

Before she could explore any of her questions, someone barged into the room.

She glanced up and saw Mayor Tomlinson standing there. His face loosened with grief when he saw Bob's body—and then he glared at Cassidy, and she knew that he somehow thought this was all her fault.

Mac couldn't be elected to fill his position soon enough.

———

CASSIDY DIDN'T GET home until after midnight, but she was wide awake when she arrived. Ty had waited up for her, a gesture that warmed her heart and made her feel so incredibly loved and valued.

Yet, despite that, her thoughts felt heavy—burdened. Almost like she was on the brink of having her perfect life here stripped away from her.

Was that what this feeling—this rising anxiety—was? Everything felt so fragile and breakable right now, like in the blink of an eye life as she knew it could shatter.

She supposed part of it was the case. There were so many moving parts to it. She'd tried to call Gilead's parents earlier, but they hadn't answered. She'd left a message but had little hope they would return her call. Most parents protected their children at all cost.

She was worried about Serena. Apprehensive about Gilead's run for mayor. Concerned about the circumstances around those dead bodies in the woods.

And anxious that the text she'd gotten meant she was living on borrowed time.

As Ty fixed her some tea, she wrapped a throw around her shoulders and stepped onto the deck, Kujo on her heels. Somehow, she always could think more easily when she was near the ocean. As she waited for Ty, she stared out into the vast darkness—darkness that seemed to have no end.

The ocean hid in the blinding nighttime. She couldn't see it, but she knew it was there. Could hear the waves. Could smell the salty air.

It reminded her that she couldn't rely only on what she could see. The reminder was good because, right now, all that was in her vision was trouble and unsettling change.

A moment later, Ty joined her, handing her a warm

cup of raspberry tea. He said nothing, just gave her space to process her day, her thoughts.

"You remember when we first met," Cassidy finally started, letting the sound of the waves crashing roll over her.

"Of course. I was driving my cousin's truck, you thought I cut you off, and then you confronted me about the bumper stickers on the back—the ones you didn't approve of." Ty smiled.

Cassidy smiled also as she replayed the day in her head. "And then later you came up behind me on the sand dune—"

"And you flipped me over your shoulder until I landed on a patch of sand spurs." He put his hands on her shoulders and leaned closer. "That's when I knew it was true love."

Cassidy turned to face him, desperately fighting the feeling that her world was beginning to crumble. "That seems like so long ago, but it was barely a year."

Ty pushed her hair back behind her shoulders before letting his hands rest on her waist. "It does, doesn't it."

"You had no idea what you were getting yourself into the first time you kissed me."

"I wouldn't change a thing, Cassidy. Well, maybe I would change the fact that so many people want you dead. But other than that . . ."

"It's been an adventure, hasn't it?"

"It really has been. Maybe I can whisk you away

somewhere for our one-year anniversary. Get away from the craziness around here."

"That would be nice. But I might need to save up my leave time in case we need to visit your mom. I know she's been doing better now but . . ."

His mom had been undergoing treatments for ovarian cancer. Though she was in remission, Cassidy knew they needed to be on call in case things changed.

"I think we could still squeeze something in," Ty said. "You make time for the things that are important, right?"

"You do. But life here is like a vacation."

"Except that you're chasing killers all the time and keeping your eye on a potentially deadly cult and trying to protect all the innocent citizens who live here. It's a big task, one where you don't get a lot of breaks."

She frowned. "It's true. But I know I'm doing what I need to be doing, Ty."

"I know you are too. I just worry about you." He wrapped his arms around her and drew her close until they were snuggled against each other. "I love you, Cassidy Chambers."

Her heart pounded with warmth. "I love you too, Ty. Always and forever."

He drew her even closer until their lips touched and Cassidy was swept away from all her worries—for a few minutes, at least.

But Cassidy would take whatever she could get.

CHAPTER SEVENTEEN

MORIAH FELT a new spring to her step as she emerged from her room the next morning. She had only one day until she got married. One day.

Then her life was going to change.

A smile stretched across her face. She couldn't wait.

She paused in the hallway, noting that Gilead's door was cracked open.

Maybe she could see him. Maybe she could steal a kiss.

Would Gilead like that? Or would he find it intrusive?

She wasn't sure.

But Moriah was going to be his wife. She shouldn't fear the man's reaction.

She stepped closer, about to knock when she caught a glimpse of Gilead.

Her eyes widened when she realized he was

changing clothes. He was mostly dressed, and his back was toward her. But he hadn't yet slipped his shirt on.

His physique captured her gaze.

His broad shoulders.

His muscular biceps.

His . . .

She sucked in a gasp.

What was that on his back? There were scars. Horrible scars.

Not scars like the burn mark on her own back. These scars ran in every direction. Almost like . . . someone had whipped him.

No. That couldn't be right.

But where would he have gotten such marks? It didn't make sense.

Gilead tugged on a shirt and then turned toward the door. As he did, Moriah slipped away. Was she too late? Had he seen her?

She didn't dare linger any longer. She darted toward the steps, her heart pounding.

She needed to prepare to meet with Serena. She needed space before she saw Gilead—space to process exactly what she'd seen.

Breakfast and the morning session were like a blur, though. She couldn't get the image of those scars out of her mind.

But before she knew it, it was time to meet Serena. She remembered Gilead's request.

I need you to find out any information on Cassidy Chambers.

The only way Moriah could do that was through talking to Serena. But even the thought of Cassidy made her stomach turn.

"Good morning, Moriah," Serena called, offering a bright smile.

Moriah nodded hello as she stepped outside the Meeting Place, wondering how the girl could be so perky. "Good morning. Let's take a walk."

Serena nodded. The girl had long, dark hair that had a wave to it, pale skin, and curious eyes. Somehow, she looked out of place in her tunic and khakis. She seemed like the kind of person who flourished while expressing herself by what she wore and how she did her makeup. Trivial things that didn't matter.

Serena would be in for a wake-up call here at the Cove.

They fell into step beside each other, walking toward the garden area.

She remembered Gilead's advice. *Make her like you. Then she'll do whatever you want. You just have to know how to handle people.*

That's not what Gilead had done to Moriah, was it?

She sucked in a quick breath at the thought. No, of course not. Why did she always have to be so full of self-doubt?

"So how do you like it here so far?" Moriah asked.

Part of her didn't care, but she couldn't show that. Like Gilead said, she needed to make Serena like her.

"It's . . . it's lovely. But different. I can't quite get used to dressing the same way and eating the same things every day. I used to sell ice cream for a living."

Moriah glanced the woman's way, surprised by her words. "Ice cream? Interesting."

"What I wouldn't give right now for a Nutty Buddy."

Moriah smiled. She hadn't thought about frozen treats in a long time. But now that Serena mentioned it . . . a Nutty Buddy would be amazing. She didn't dare share that out loud.

"So, you and Dietrich are close?" Moriah continued. She pulled her tunic tighter around her neck. The day wasn't cold, but the breeze was. She wasn't sure she'd ever get used to the cooler seasons here on the island.

"He's just great, isn't he?" Serena practically glowed as she said the words.

"I don't know him well, especially since he doesn't live here at the Cove." Moriah had always wondered about that. Gilead had told her those who didn't live at the Cove were scouts. They were the ones actively recruiting and trying to bring people into their group. Those people seemed to be some of the ones Gilead trusted the most.

"He's handsome and smart," Serena told her. "What else can I say?"

"And he talked to you about being here and all it involves?"

"He talked to me about finding my true purpose in life. He pointed out the emptiness in my eyes and how I should be living to the fullest instead."

"Gilead is great at speaking truth into our lives, isn't he?"

"Oh, he's wonderful. I finally feel like I have a reason to wake up each day. I know now that I was put here on this earth so I could learn under Gilead's teaching. He's going to change me. I can feel it."

Moriah's throat burned as a question fought to get out. Should she bring this subject up or not? She would, she decided. She was brave. Had courage. Strength.

"Do you miss your life outside this place?" Moriah asked. "Certainly you have friends here on the island who are worried."

Moriah was specifically thinking about Cassidy. Thinking about how Gilead had asked her to find out more information on the woman. She couldn't let him down.

"I do," Serena admitted. "But the sacrifice is worth the cause."

"Do you have family on the island?"

"Just my aunt Skye and her boyfriend, Austin. He's not family—yet. But he will be."

"Being here in Gilead's Cove, you might miss their wedding, whenever it happens."

Serena frowned, as if she hadn't thought about that.

"Even if I do, I'll be there with them in heart. Besides, I'm not trapped here at Gilead's Cove, right? I do have the right to come and go when I want."

"In theory, yes. But it's not smiled upon. Especially when you're new."

Serena rubbed her throat, as if it had tightened. "I see."

Moriah had to keep Serena talking and see if she could find out any information. "So, do you know that police chief here on the island?" Moriah ventured.

Serena glanced at her, surprise in her gaze. "Cassidy? No, we're not really friends. I bought the ice cream truck from her is all."

"The police chief used to drive an ice cream truck?" Moriah wondered about the story behind that.

"I know it sounds strange. But Lantern Beach can be a strange place."

"I guess so." They paused by the garden area. Though it was early in the season, the garden still had to be tended. That was what Ruth always said, and Ruth should know since the garden was one of her areas. "What do you know about the woman?"

"The police chief?" Serena shrugged. "Not much. Only that she's great. She's smart, pretty, loyal. Her husband is what dreams are made of. I would love to have her life.

A flash of jealousy seared through her. Moriah needed to know more about this new enemy so she could combat her. Moriah wasn't as naïve as she'd once been, and she was ready to fight to get what she wanted. What she deserved.

Moriah swallowed deeply before saying, "Funny, I heard she's not the faithful kind of woman."

Serena's eyes widened. "Cassidy? She's definitely faithful . . . I mean, from what I know about her. I've only talked to her a few times, though. What's with all the questions?"

Moriah didn't think Serena sounded convincing— more like she was trying to protect her friend, Cassidy. "She seems to oppose our group here, so I just wanted to know what it was about her background that might cause that."

Serena shrugged. "She probably sees Gilead's Cove as a threat to the island. A lot of locals do."

"Why would we be a threat?" Moriah let out a little laugh at the absurdity of the statement.

Serena cast a quick glance at her but said nothing. Instead, after an awkward moment of silence, she cleared her throat. "Say, as I was trying to sleep last night, I saw three men walking around the compound. What's their job?"

"Walking around at night? Probably just security." Why was she bringing this up? The subject change irritated her.

"But they went out a gate and into the woods," Serena continued.

Moriah's heart thumped in her chest. Was Serena correct? Why would men be leaving at night? "I don't know what you're talking about. Besides, you should mind your own business."

Serena shrugged, as if unaffected by her scolding. "I was just curious."

"Well, curiosity can have consequences. You'd be wise to put those notions aside and concentrate solely on your own well-being right now."

"My own well-being?" Serena stared at her.

Moriah realized what she'd said. "Your own spiritual growth."

Serena nodded. "Of course."

"Now, let's keep walking."

CHAPTER EIGHTEEN

THE NEXT MORNING, Cassidy jerked up in bed. Her phone buzzed on the nightstand, pulling her from an engulfing, all-too-realistic dream where she'd been running from a faceless shadow. Her heart raced as the vivid images pummeled her mind.

It had felt so real.

She'd felt so threatened.

So in danger.

"Cassidy, do you need to get that?" Ty turned over in bed and stuffed his pillow beneath his head as his sleepy gaze fell on her.

Her phone, she remembered.

Her personal phone had been buzzing.

She raked a hand through her mane of hair and grabbed her cell. But it was too late.

She'd missed the call. She glanced at the number

and saw it said private. She sighed, putting the phone back down.

"Who was it?" Ty asked, draping his arm across her.

"I don't know. They'll leave a message if it's important."

He pulled her closer to his warm body, and she melted there. During the in-between seasons, it always felt cold in the cottage. Too warm for the heat to come on. Too cool for the AC.

If only she and Ty could stay here all day, just relaxing and enjoying each other's company.

But all her pressing concerns flooded back to her.

She forced her eyes open again and saw that it was almost eight o'clock.

A groan escaped from her, and she pulled the soft blanket up tighter around her neck. Sunlight streamed in through the blinds, and Kujo lay at her feet.

"What?" Ty murmured into her hair.

"I have to get to work."

"Call in sick?" He didn't release his hold on her.

"I wish I could."

"Why is your heart racing so fast? I can feel it thumping against my chest."

"Bad dream."

"Want to tell me about it?"

Cassidy turned over and ran her hand along his face, soaking in his features—his handsome features that she'd be quite content to stare at all day. His scruffy beard, intelligent and sometimes mischievous eyes, his messy brown hair. She still marveled sometimes that she'd found someone like him.

She remembered his question. "There's nothing to tell. In my dream, a shadow was chasing me, and I . . . I was certain I was going to die."

Her attempt at a lighthearted tone fell flat.

"That doesn't sound like nothing."

Cassidy shrugged. "It seemed real and got my adrenaline going, I suppose."

Ty kissed her forehead. "Those are the worst. What do you think it means?"

She didn't have to think about it long.

"What if I can't figure everything out, Ty?" she whispered. "What if I can't make things right? What if Gilead is elected and Serena is really converted and . . . I could go on."

"You'll figure things out, Cassidy. You always do."

She wished she was as convinced. "This case has my stomach all twisted in knots."

"By this case, you mean the dead bodies in the woods?"

"I mean all of it combined and linked. The bodies in the woods, the men who shot at us from the boat . . ."

"Just take a deep breath. It will come together. It always does."

Cassidy really hoped Ty was right.

Just then, her phone buzzed again. Maybe the earlier caller had left a message.

Hesitantly, she pulled herself from Ty's warm

embrace and grabbed her phone. Her blurry gaze hit the screen.

Everyone could find out Cady Matthews is really Cassidy Chambers. Just one post from me, and your life will be ruined. Don't forget it.

———

"I DON'T LIKE THIS." Ty's chest squeezed with anger.

Cassidy buttoned her shirt, preparing herself to go into work. "I don't like it either. But what am I supposed to do? Cower inside indefinitely?"

"Someone knows about your past. They got your phone number. They're probably watching you and your every move." He stopped behind Cassidy and put his hands on her shoulders as she looked in the mirror.

She straightened the collar to her police uniform. "I know that. I promise you I do. But I'm not going to be bullied. If I'm exposed, then I'm exposed. Nothing I do is going to change that."

Cassidy's words might be true, but that didn't mean Ty liked them. One person shouldn't have this much power over someone else. These threats . . . they had to stop.

"Let me go into work with you and be a second sets of eyes," he said.

Cassidy turned toward him and offered a sad smile. "I appreciate that. I really do. But you have work to do here. I'll call you if I need you."

Hope House . . . Ty still hadn't told Cassidy about his financial struggles with the nonprofit. He knew he should but . . . he just hadn't found the right opportunity, he supposed.

"What is it, Ty?" Cassidy tilted her head as she studied his face. "What's that look?"

"I have a look?"

She nodded. "I can see it in your eyes. What aren't you telling me?"

He sighed and stepped back, lowering himself onto the edge of the bed. He wasn't going to bring it up now, but . . ."I'm out of money, Cassidy."

She lowered herself beside him, a knot between her eyes as she faced him. "What do you mean?"

"I mean, all the added expenses from the storm . . . it depleted so much of the savings for the nonprofit. I need to purchase the plane tickets for the guys to come here, but I don't have the funds."

"Oh, Ty . . . why didn't you tell me? I had no idea."

"You have so much going on, Cassidy. I didn't want to add anything else to your plate."

She ran her hand across his face. "But you're my husband. I'm supposed to help you carry your burdens."

He squeezed her hand, touched by her compassion. "I know. I was hoping things would turn around. One of the corporations that donated last year said they would give again this year. But then their stocks plunged and . . . well, they never followed through."

"There have to be other corporations that would help."

"I'm sure there are. And I just need to get on the phone and start calling them. I've been focusing so much time on getting these cabanas up and running for the center that I really let this fall by the wayside. I just assumed the money would come in, but it didn't. It's my fault, and no one else's."

"You can't do everything, Ty. Maybe you should see about getting some help."

He nodded. "I've thought about it."

"But you rarely have time to do anything extra because you're always so busy looking after me." Cassidy frowned.

"Hey." Ty cupped her face with his hands. "This isn't your fault."

"What are you going to do? You can't cancel the next session. Maybe I can talk to my parents—"

"Your mom isn't exactly speaking with you since you turned down her job offer," Ty reminded. "Besides, any contact you have with your past puts you at a bigger risk of being discovered. I want to do things on my own."

She seemed to hesitantly nod. "We'll think of something, Ty."

"Thanks for your support, Cassidy." He leaned forward and kissed her softly. "But now you need to get to work. We'll talk more about this later."

"Yes, we will." She stood and gave him a look that clearly stated this conversation wasn't done.

CHAPTER NINETEEN

AS CASSIDY STEPPED into her office at the station, her phone rang. She glanced back. Where was Melva today?

It didn't matter.

She closed her door, sat down, and then grabbed the receiver.

"Chief Cassidy Chambers," she answered. "How can I help you?"

Silence answered.

Tension pinched at her spine. Was this another threat? A prank call? A waste of her time?

"Hello?" she repeated. She gave the caller one more opportunity before she hung up.

Silence again.

Just as Cassidy pulled the phone away from her ear, a feeble voice sounded on the other line.

"You can't tell him I called."

Cassidy shoved the phone against her ear. "I'm sorry? Who is this?"

"You can't tell him I called," a woman whispered. "Promise me."

"I can't promise anything until I know—"

"This is Winona Becker. Gerrard's mom. And I'm hanging up in three seconds unless I know I can trust you."

Cassidy's pulse spiked. She couldn't mess up this opportunity. "You can trust me."

Mrs. Becker remained silent a moment. "I wasn't going to call you back, you know."

"But you did. Why?" Cassidy leaned back in her seat, bracing herself for whatever this conversation might hold. She hoped she might finally get some answers.

"My husband doesn't know I'm making this call. He's in the shower, so I don't have long."

The woman still didn't answer her questions. Yet, despite that, Cassidy's interest only grew. "Why are you calling, Mrs. Becker?"

"I got your message last night. I intended on ignoring it." Mrs. Becker's voice sounded soft and gentle, like she was nurturing and sweet. "But then Gerrard called."

Cassidy sucked in a breath. "He called you last night?"

"That's right. He threatened that I shouldn't speak to anyone."

"Your son threatened you?" The man was even more despicable than Cassidy had assumed.

"That's right," Mrs. Becker whispered. "He's always cared too much about his image. He knows that I know the truth and that I could ruin him."

Cassidy knew she didn't have much time and that she needed to ask the important questions before it was too late. "What do you know the truth about, Mrs. Becker?"

She held her breath as she waited for Mrs. Becker's response. As she did, she turned to her computer and pulled up the woman's picture from social media. She appeared to be in her fifties with dark hair, a slim build, and kind eyes.

Not the kind of person Cassidy had necessarily pictured. She looked too normal. Cassidy's intrigue only grew.

"He's not right in the head," Mrs. Becker said quietly. "But most people don't see it."

"Why don't you think he's right in the head?"

"He's always been a bit of a narcissist. But something changed in him after the Middle East."

"Why was he in the Middle East?" Gilead had told Cassidy he'd been there, but she wanted more details, more answers. She wanted to know if the story he'd told her matched the one he'd told his mom.

"When his church pastoring position failed, he found a job as a contractor. He was stationed overseas for three years. He was never the same after that. He was . . . obsessed, I suppose you'd say."

"Obsessed with what?"

"He claimed to have found a scroll with this undiscovered book of the Bible that I'd never heard of. I could see this new purpose in his gaze. He started an online movement and gained followers. Not long after that, he moved to West Virginia to begin doing these revivals."

Cassidy absorbed everything Mrs. Becker told her. "So he really feels as if he was called by God? You really think he found this scroll?"

"Of course not. My son feeds on influencing other people. It's a game to him."

Cassidy's breath caught. Maybe she was finally on to something. "What do you mean?"

Mrs. Becker hesitated. "Look, in high school Gerrard and some of his friends talked another kid into drinking too much alcohol too fast. The boy died. It was horrible."

"I'm sorry to hear that." Cassidy couldn't even imagine what the boy's family had been through. And to think Gerrard played a part in it . . . the reveal didn't really surprise Cassidy. But this was the kind of information she needed to get a better idea about what made Gilead/Gerrard tick.

"There was a trial, but Gerrard was never named as a defendant. His friends were. Two of them went to jail for seven years."

Cassidy's jaw clenched. How had the man managed that? Even at a young age, Gilead knew how to get his way, didn't he? "How did your son get off the hook?"

"He has this way about him where he can twist people's words. Where he can put ideas in their heads. I guess he left the party before the police arrived, and no one could remember him being there during the hazing incident. But one of these boys' moms called me. She told me the truth. The problem was that there was no evidence. It was like that with Rhonda, as well."

"Who's Rhonda?"

"She was his wife. They met and married while he was in seminary. I saw the bruises on her. When I mentioned it to Gerrard, he insisted she was clumsy. It wasn't long after that he distanced himself from me."

A chill washed over Cassidy. The news didn't surprise her. It only confirmed what she already knew.

"How did that affect your relationship with your son?"

"Well, I still loved him. Of course. But I couldn't shake the feeling that there was something troubling about him. I hoped he would straighten himself out."

"Did he?"

"It's . . . it's hard to say. He got that job at the church and—" Mrs. Becker suddenly stopped, and silence stretched.

Cassidy drew in a quick breath, desperate to hear more. Desperate for Mrs. Becker to talk more, to finish what she'd started to reveal. "What were you saying, Mrs. Becker?"

"I'm sorry," she rushed. "I can't talk anymore. My husband is getting out of the shower. Please don't tell anyone I spoke with you."

"Mrs. Becker—"

"I have to go. But, Chief, be careful."

"Why?"

"Because I fear if anyone stands in Gerrard's way, he'll kill them."

Then the line went dead.

———

CASSIDY'S THOUGHTS wouldn't settle and instead spun like a frenzied top. She replayed her conversation with Winona Becker over and over again. Each time, her chills deepened.

If Gilead's own mother feared that he'd kill anyone in his way, then Cassidy knew her qualms weren't unfounded. She was dealing with a dangerous man.

Cassidy also suspected that Gilead had threatened anyone else from his past who might reveal his true identity. But why? What was he trying to hide? What was so important that he'd changed his name?

She had no idea. Instead, she tapped her pen against her desk as the thoughts turned over in her head.

When the state crime lab called fifteen minutes later, she welcomed the distraction.

"Chief, we got a match on those ballistics from the bullets that were fired at you."

Cassidy sat up straight. "Let's hear it."

"They actually match a weapon from another crime on the island two years ago. It was a dispute between two neighbors over the use of some property. Things escalated and shots were fired by both parties, though neither ever did any serious time for the crime."

"And?"

"And the person who owned the gun . . . his name is a little different. Moby Rick."

Cassidy leaned back. Moby? So the man was connected after all.

"Thanks so much for the update," Cassidy said. "I'll let Agent Abbott with the NCSBI know."

She stood. Maybe she finally had a lead. She grabbed Dane from his office to go with her.

"We're getting a lot of calls, Chief," Melva told her on the way out the door.

The woman had finally shown up. Apparently, she'd had a water leak at her house, and she appeared even more high-strung than usual as she sucked in shallow breaths and manically straightened some papers on her desk.

"Tell everyone I have no comment. Besides, there's nothing to say yet. It's too early."

"Yes, Chief." Melva nodded quickly.

Cassidy filled Dane in as they climbed into her vehicle. Ten minutes later, they pulled up to the little tackle shop Moby owned. It was practically a shack with a covered porch and dirt parking lot. But the place had its regulars.

Cassidy and Dane stepped inside the space, the scent of bait and fish filling the air.

Moby looked up. Saw her.

And then he took off in a run.

CHAPTER TWENTY

CASSIDY SPRINTED AFTER MOBY. The man was faster than she'd assumed. His short legs and small frame moved quickly and with an agility she temporarily envied.

"Dane, go around the other side of the building," she yelled.

He nodded and did as she ordered. Hopefully, between the two of them, they could catch this guy.

Moby didn't have but so many places to go. Water surrounded the back side of his property, trees stretched on either side of the land, and then rows and rows of beach houses lined the area beyond.

Cassidy spotted Moby hurdle a fence in the distance then head toward the trees.

Her legs burned as she pushed herself as hard as she could and hurdled the same fence.

When she was only two feet away from the man, she lunged toward him.

Her body collided with his, and they both tumbled to the sandy—but root-laced—ground.

"You had to do that the hard way, didn't you?" Cassidy muttered, an ache in her still-bruised ribs. She had to remind herself she wasn't up to speed yet after a nasty confrontation last week. It would take a while for her ribs to recover.

Moby grumbled something under his breath as Cassidy cuffed him.

Dane stopped beside them, still trying to catch his breath as well. "Good job, Chief."

"Thanks." She pulled Moby to his feet and scowled. "Now, we have a lot to talk about."

"I had nothing to do with those bodies." Moby's nostrils flared, but he didn't look angry. No, the man was scared, if anything.

He had a small stature, longish light-brown hair, and the faintest shadow of a thin mustache.

"If you had nothing to do with those bodies, then why did you run?" Cassidy edged him back so she could see his face. "And why do you think I'm here about those bodies?"

The sunlight cut through a nearby tree, glaring at the man and causing him to squint uncomfortably. She didn't make any effort to block the light.

"What else would you be here for?" Moby scowled at her again. "And I ran because I know you think I did, and you're not gunna believe me, whatever I tell you. I don't know how those sinkers got around those people's necks."

"I have a feeling there's something you're not telling me, and you need to start talking, Moby. Now." Cassidy's sympathy had disappeared when the ache in her ribs materialized. "Or do I need to take you down to the station?"

He patted his hands in the air, as if trying to tamp down the situation. "No, I'll talk. I promise. I'll talk. I just don't want to go to jail."

"Your gun was used to shoot at me and my men a couple days ago, Moby," Cassidy said. "Can you explain that? Maybe you even own a skiff. Maybe you were on board."

Moby's brown eyes widened, and he glanced at Dane, as if expecting him to admit this was all a joke. Dane only gave him a cold stare back.

"My gun?" Moby's voice cracked. "Is that what this is about? It was stolen six months ago."

Cassidy clenched her teeth, not ready to believe him yet. "How was it stolen, Moby?"

He shrugged. "I wish I knew. I kept it behind the counter here at Moby Rick's. One day, it was gone."

Irritation pinched at Cassidy's spine. "And you never reported it?"

He shrugged again. "No, I didn't. Figured I'd get in trouble again, just like last time."

"And by last time, you mean when you shot at your

neighbor?" Cassidy had read the police report before she'd come.

His face reddened, and he let out a few choice words. "That man was crazy. I was just defending my property. I have that right, you know. He parked his old beat-up car on my land, and he was going to leave it there to rust. It was an eyesore, and he was being unreasonable."

Cassidy and Dane exchanged a look. Moby might present himself as an upstanding citizen, but he not only had that incident on his rap sheet, he'd also been arrested for driving under the influence. All of that was proof he didn't always make wise decisions.

"We're not here to talk about that," Cassidy finally said. "We're here to talk about your connection to this crime. Your gun was used to shoot at us, and sinkers you sell here at your shop were found on the bodies. That's what I want you to explain. That's two connections with you, and it doesn't look good."

"What? I would have never used my gun to shoot someone," Moby said. "I mean, unless they were trespassing on my property. But, like I said, my gun was stolen."

"You need to start explaining and sharing some more details." Cassidy didn't bother to keep the impatience out of her voice.

Moby let out a long sigh and stared off in the distance a moment. Cassidy glanced back and saw an oversized truck pulling up in the parking lot of the tackle shop, the front and back loaded down with fishing gear and coolers.

Moby was losing some money right now, but he didn't seem to be in a hurry to return to his business.

"I met someone about six months ago." His jaw clenched, as if he was bothered by the memory. "I'm not saying she has any connection. But maybe she does."

"Tell us more," Cassidy said.

"I met a girl. A *woman*, I suppose is more accurate." He made a face, reminding Cassidy of a second grader who poked girls in the ribcage to flirt with them. "She was about six years younger than me."

"How old are you?" Dane asked.

"Thirty-two."

Dane nodded. "Keep going."

Moby raked a hand through his mullet and frowned. "So, I met this girl. She came into my shop. She'd just come to the island, and she said she wanted to experience island life to the fullest."

"And this ties in with your gun somehow?" Cassidy was having trouble figuring out how this was connected, and she really hated it when people wasted her time.

"Let me finish." He squinted again before glancing back at his shop and watching the truck with his potential customer pull away.

"You have a name?" Dane stood in front of him, blocking his view of the store.

"It was . . . Reagan."

Cassidy sucked in a breath at the familiar name. "Reagan what?"

"I don't remember, but it reminded me of food and being hungry."

"Craven?" Cassidy asked.

"Yes! That's it. Reagan Craven."

Cassidy tried not to show her excitement at the connection. "What did she look like?"

"She had red hair. Kind of pretty. Then again, I'm not too picky."

"Tell me more about your interaction with her," Cassidy said.

"She'd never fished before, and she wanted to learn. She asked if I ever did any charter fishing trips. I told her I did—in the evenings, after the shop closed."

Cassidy soaked in all the information, ready to start connecting the dots. "Did you take her out?"

"I did. That very evening, as a matter of fact." He rocked his head up in a nod and left his chin raised with something resembling pride.

"Was she here alone on the island?" Dane asked. "Or did she come with someone?"

"As far as I knew, she was by herself. I didn't really ask her."

That was too bad, Cassidy mused. "And was that your only interaction with her?"

Moby frowned as if guilty and rolled his shoulders. "No, it wasn't. We had dinner together the next two nights."

And the plot thickens . . . "And then?"

Moby shrugged. "And then nothing. She didn't answer my calls. I figured she either left or met someone else. It was just as well, honestly."

"Why is that?" Dane asked.

"She wasn't really my type. And I could tell she had a lot of . . . what do people call it? Baggage, I guess. But it was fun while it lasted."

"How about the sinkers?" Cassidy asked. "And the gun? How do those things fit with what you're telling us?"

"Reagan liked the anchor sinkers. Liked them a lot. Said she needed an anchor in her life, and that they reminded her of the fact. She bought a few."

Cassidy scowled this time. "That would have been helpful to know when I asked you earlier, Moby."

"I just didn't want to get in trouble."

"Reagan buying sinkers doesn't equate with you getting in trouble," Dane reminded him.

"Then my gun disappeared. I think she might have taken it." Moby's cheeks reddened, like the whole incident embarrassed him. "Actually, I think her friend might have taken it."

"So she did have a friend." More irritation rose in Cassidy. Why couldn't this guy give a straight answer? "You know, maybe we should take you in to the station."

"No! I'm talking. I promise, I am. It just takes me a while to get to my point." Moby cleared his throat. "I think she might have stolen it because she distracted me at the back of the store, acting all sweet and all. When I came out, this guy who was all tatted up was near the register. He was a scary-looking dude."

"How so?" Dane asked. "Just the tattoos?"

"He was big. Kind of like Jimmy James, only meaner. They didn't think I noticed, but Reagan and this guy . . . their eyes connected. I saw something there. He left, and then a few minutes later, so did Reagan. That's when I noticed my gun was gone."

"And you didn't try to find her to ask her about it?" Dane said.

"I didn't know where she lived. She never told me. And no, she didn't give me her phone number. Whenever we spoke, it was because she came into the shop."

"Did she ever mention anything about Gilead's Cove?"

Moby remained silent in thought for a minute. "Not really. But she did say something about discovering a new way of living."

"Did she call it 'the Cause,' by chance?" Cassidy asked.

"Maybe. I can't say for sure. Now, did I tell you enough?"

Cassidy nodded, feeling like they were making some progress, at least. She'd take that over nothing. And she'd be keeping a very close eye on Lantern Beach's local tackle shop owner.

CHAPTER TWENTY-ONE

AFTER CASSIDY WROTE up her report on Moby, she headed over to Lisa's for Mac's impromptu political rally.

Her friend had fixed many of her signature dishes, even her grilled cheese with peaches, and the place smelled heavenly—like bacon and freshly baked bread and warm chocolate.

Cassidy paused at the door and glanced around. The place had been decorated with red, white, and blue streamers. Local musician Carter Denver played his guitar and sang patriotic tunes in the corner. Meanwhile, Mac stood in the middle of the crowd, impressing everyone with his ability to quote the alphabet in various different ways—forward, backward, skipping letters, etc. It was his parlor trick, so to speak, and people loved it.

A grin spread across her face. A lot of people were

already here to support Mac, and that realization thrilled her. Mac deserved the win this election. No one cared about Lantern Beach as much as he did.

"Hey, you." Ty appeared beside her and planted a quick kiss on her cheek.

"Hey, hon. How's it going?"

Ty looked out across the crowd. "This is small town goodness at its finest."

"I agree. Honestly, I can't imagine Mac losing this election. He's just what the town needs." Cassidy winced and touched her side.

Ty studied her expression, his full attention suddenly on her. "Did you hurt your ribs again?"

"I'm fine. Just a little run-in with Moby Rick."

"Moby? The man seems harmless. I can't see him doing anything malicious just for the sake of being malicious."

"I agree. My gut tells me he's innocent. But he did have a few interesting things to share." Cassidy told him about their conversation.

"Sounds like you're getting closer to answers, Cassidy."

"I can only hope so."

Several people stopped Cassidy and chatted with her. Right before she was about to leave, a middle-aged woman who looked vaguely familiar sidled up beside Cassidy and whispered, "Can I talk to you?"

"Of course. What about?"

The woman glanced around, as if making sure no

one else was listening. "It's about that girl here on the island who stole the gun."

Cassidy tensed at her words. "How did you hear about that?"

"Moby is my nephew—my sister's boy. He told me that you came in today. He . . . well, he's always liked to talk to me about things, and he was very upset."

This conversation had just taken a very interesting turn. "Okay. What's your name again?"

The blonde, who still sported eighties-style big hair, frowned. "It's Barbara. I own the toy store down on the boardwalk, All for Fun and Fun for All."

That's where Cassidy had seen her before. "And what is it that you need to tell me?"

Barbara frowned, her skin sagging with the expression. "I think I spoke with that woman once."

———

CASSIDY GUIDED Barbara into the back of the restaurant, where they could talk privately. In the distance, they could hear people murmuring and Carter Denver playing.

"Please, tell me what you know," Cassidy started. "Anything will help."

Barbara rubbed her hands on her arms. "I think this woman came into my shop. I only remember because she had red hair, and I knew Moby had gone out with someone with red hair. If you've never lived in a small town, you don't realize that people are connected and related. I don't think she had any clue I was Moby's aunt."

"I'm sure there are a lot of redheads who vacation here. Why do you think this woman is the same one we found at the scene?"

"I know it sounds strange, but I just can't stop thinking about her." Barbara's face scrunched together as if distressed. "I think she's the one."

"Keep going. Tell me why."

"I don't know. There was just something about her. She looked scared, I suppose."

"Why did she come in?"

"She was looking at stuffed animals."

"Did she buy any?"

"She actually bought ten. She said it was for her little sister in Kentucky."

Reagan's father had said she was the only child. So either Reagan had lied to Barbara or it wasn't Reagan who'd come into the toy store. However, Reagan had been from Kentucky.

Cassidy would still hear the woman out, just in case.

"Anything special about these stuffed animals?" And, if Reagan had bought them, where were they now? They still hadn't determined where Reagan had been staying on the island—not unless Abbott knew something that Cassidy didn't.

"They were all on the large size, I suppose. Mostly

teddy bears and stuffed horses. I think one was a zebra."

"What exactly was so memorable about this woman other than the purchase and her red hair?" There was something else here. Cassidy felt sure of it.

"She was with a man," Barbara said. "He had ruddy skin and a weird name. I didn't want to tell Moby because I thought it might break his heart. That boy's had zero luck in love."

Cassidy's pulse spiked. A weird name? Was there anyone from Gilead's Cove with weird names? Gilead himself maybe? But he didn't have ruddy skin.

"A weird name like Gilead?"

Barbara shook her head, her forehead cinched. "No, it was longer. It reminded me of a character from the Andy Griffith show."

It had been forever since Cassidy had thought about that show. What were the characters' names? "Opie?"

The lines on Barbara's forehead grew deeper. "No, it was longer. And it started with a B."

"Barney maybe?" As the name left her lips, Cassidy sucked in a breath. No, it wasn't Barney. It was . . . "Barnabas. Was it Barnabas?"

Barbara snapped her fingers and nodded. "Yes, I think that was it. She was with a man named Barnabas."

Cassidy felt a rush of excitement at the new lead. "Anything else?"

"There was another man outside. He was big and kind of scary looking."

Was that the man who'd stolen Moby's gun? It sure sounded like it.

"As the three of them left, I heard them say something about going down to the docks." Barbara frowned. "The whole thing was strange, Chief. Very strange. I've had a bad feeling ever since then."

Maybe Cassidy finally had enough to get that search warrant for Gilead's Cove. That's where Barnabas had lived, and maybe the dead man would somehow provide some answers.

CHAPTER TWENTY-TWO

____

"SO GILEAD'S mom actually called back?" Ty repeated as he headed down the road with Cassidy toward Gilead's Cove with her search warrant in hand.

His wife looked downright determined as her hands gripped the wheel and her gaze focused straight ahead. She was definitely on a mission.

"It's disturbing, to put it lightly, to hear a mother so afraid of her own son," Cassidy told him. "It's left me with an uneasy feeling since I talked to her."

"And she did confirm Gilead was in the Middle East?" Ty's breath hitched as he waited for Cassidy's response. He felt desperate to put together pieces— pieces that he couldn't quite see, yet he knew they were there. That Gilead had some connection to his past.

"She did. At least, that's the story Gilead told her. That would put him there the same time as you. I wish I'd had time to ask more questions."

Ty stared out the window and let her words sink in. Anthony Gilead was in the Middle East at the same time Ty had served as a SEAL on several missions in the area. How had their paths crossed?

"I don't like this," Ty muttered.

"Believe me, no one does. At least, I have this warrant now. Maybe we'll discover something."

"We can hope."

She pulled up to the gate and pushed a button there. Several minutes later, a man sauntered up to the guard station and poked his head out the window.

"Can I help you?" the tunic-wearing man asked.

"I'm Chief Chambers with the Lantern Beach PD. I have a warrant to search a trailer here on your property."

The man took the paper from her and read the words there, nodding slowly. "I see. I'm going to need to run this past someone in charge."

"This is a legal document. I don't need anyone's approval."

"I understand. Could you just give me a minute?"

Cassidy looked as if she considered telling him no, but instead she nodded. "You have four minutes to get back here before I use other means. Understand?"

"Yes, ma'am." He hurried off in the direction he'd come from.

Cassidy glanced over at Ty and released a long, pent-up breath. "I really hope we find something."

"I really hope we do also. I know it would put a lot of people here on the island at ease."

True to his word, the man returned a few minutes later, handed back the search warrant, and opened the gate. "Come on in. Kaleb said he would meet you at the end of the lane."

"Not Gilead?" Cassidy asked.

"No, he's not available right now."

"I see. Thank you for your cooperation." Cassidy pulled into the compound.

Ty had been inside Gilead's Cove a few times already, but every time the place gave him the creeps. There was just something about it that felt off, that reminded him of a terrorist compound where innocents had been tricked into a life of extremism. Ty would know—one of his missions had been at one of those very locations.

Kaleb Walker stood in the distance, waiting for them. Cassidy parked in front of him, and they climbed out. Kaleb was in his thirties, with a square face and eyes that always appeared unsettled. The man seemed out of place here at the compound. He was too educated and smart to be here.

Then again, even educated and smart people could be lost and looking for purpose. The reality remained that most of the people here at Gilead's Cove were from low socioeconomic backgrounds and had histories that included substance abuse and other problems. They fit a certain profile.

"Chief," Kaleb said before nodding at Ty. "Ty."

Cassidy held up the warrant. "I need to see the space where Barnabas was staying."

"Of course," Kaleb said. "Right this way. However, I thought you already searched it after his untimely death."

"I did," Cassidy said. "And now I need to see it again."

They followed him down a sandy path until they reached a particularly rundown RV located on the edge of the property near the water.

"This is where Barnabas kept his things. We haven't cleaned it out yet, though we were preparing to do so to make room for new guests we have coming," Kaleb said. "You came at just the right time."

"Thank you," Cassidy told him.

Ty followed her inside the dingy space. How anyone could live here amazed him—or maybe *disturbed* was a better word. Mold splotched the walls, and the whole place smelled musty. Trash littered the floor—old food wrappers and even a banana peel.

Somehow, that surprised him. Ty didn't know the ins and outs of this compound, but he guessed the residents were on a strict regime. Barnabas had either broken the rules or had been given special privileges. In fact, during a previous case a gas station attendant had told them that Barnabas often came in for a Mountain Dew and Snickers bar.

"Why are you investigating Barnabas? He's dead." Kaleb stepped in behind them and closed the door.

"He may be connected with another crime on the island," Cassidy said as she pulled on some gloves.

"Like I said, he's dead," Kaleb repeated.

"Maybe this crime happened before he died."

Kaleb nodded slowly and uncertainly. "I see."

"How much do you monitor what goes on here in the trailers?" Cassidy asked.

"For newbies?" Kaleb asked. "Quite a bit. For someone like Barnabas? Not so much. He was one of Gilead's trusted few."

"As are you," Ty pointed out.

Kaleb nodded again. "That's correct. I am also considered a part of the inner circle."

Cassidy moved cushions and anything else that wasn't stationary, trying to get a look beneath.

"What are you searching for?" Kaleb asked. "Maybe I can help."

"I'll know it when I see it."

"Really, none of us come here with much."

"So I hear." Cassidy moved a mattress.

"I am curious, however, about why you may think Barnabas is connected with some other crime." Kaleb crossed his arms and waited for her response.

"And I'm curious about what you know about Gilead."

"Touché." Kaleb shrugged in surrender.

Cassidy put down the mattress and paused, her hands on her hips as she glanced around.

"Nothing?" Kaleb asked, a touch of smugness in his voice. "Just as I suspected."

"I'm not done yet." Cassidy gave the man a pointed look.

Ty smiled. He loved his wife's tenacity and willingness to go above and beyond.

She picked up a pillow on a stiff couch and squeezed it. Her expression changed as she did.

"Did you hear that?" she asked him.

"That crinkling sound?" Ty confirmed.

She nodded. "Can I see your knife?"

He took it from his pocket, pulled the blade out, and handed it to her. "Here you go."

Carefully, she sliced into the side of the throw pillow. Then she reached into the stuffing, and her hand emerged . . . with a bag of white powder.

"Is that what I think it is?" Ty's eyes widened, and he cocked his head.

Cassidy nodded grimly. "I suspect this is flakka."

Maybe they finally had another answer.

———

CASSIDY BOUGHT herself more time by asking Kaleb to escort Ty to the Meeting Place to look at a storage area that Barnabas kept there. Before he left, Cassidy had whispered to him to keep his eyes open for Serena. That was the number one reason she'd asked him to leave. It was a great excuse to look for their friend. But the second reason was to get Kaleb away from here so she could process the scene.

Cassidy held the bag of white powder in her hands, her stomach sinking.

Flakka was the drug of choice for DH-7. It had turned up in an earlier crime here on the island as well, so she knew Gilead's Cove had some connection with the hallucinogenic drug that made people act like they'd lost their minds—or like zombies.

Memories rushed back to Cassidy again. Memories of the things people had done to get their hands on this drug.

A bag this size easily would be worth a hundred thousand on the black market.

But how did this fit her current situation? How was Barnabas connected to those human remains? How was flakka connected?

How about the gunmen? Were they from Gilead's Cove? Had they somehow stolen Moby's gun and, along with those sinkers, used the items to purposely mislead the police?

She had so many questions.

As the door closed behind Cassidy, she turned. "Back so soon?"

But all the blood left her face when she realized it wasn't Ty standing there. No, it was Anthony Gilead.

Cassidy was an officer of the law. She had a gun on her.

But still, being in this secluded place alone with the man sent shivers through her.

Gilead smiled and stepped closer. He was dressed in a lightweight beige sweater and designer jeans. His dark hair had been gelled away from his face, and he had a trendy five o'clock shadow.

He was quite a contrast to everyone else at the Cove.

"Well, if it isn't Cassidy Chambers," he crooned.

Cassidy squared her shoulders and stared back at him. "Anthony Gilead. I thought you were away. That's what the man at the front gate told us."

"I was. But I'm back now."

"Campaigning again?"

"No, I'm getting ready for my wedding, actually."

Cassidy sucked in a breath. "Your wedding?"

She knew it was coming. She'd heard that Gilead was marrying Moriah Roberts. Cassidy had just hoped that after her last talk with the woman she had changed her mind. Apparently, that had been wishful thinking.

Cassidy took a step back, anxious to put some space between herself and the man. This RV already felt too small.

"Yes, tomorrow is the big day," Gilead said.

"Well, I hope your new wife fares better than your first one. And your second one, for that matter."

He stepped closer, his eyes dark and hard yet curious. "I like your directness, Cassidy."

"It's Chief Chambers." Cassidy glanced behind him. Though she knew she could handle herself, she couldn't wait until Ty got back.

An empty smile stretched across Gilead's face. "That's right, Chief Chambers. You really do look lovely today. Your bruises are healing nicely from the incident a week or so ago."

"What are you doing here, Gilead?" Her heart pounded out of control at his nearness—and at the threatening undertones surrounding him. Cassidy could feel the danger around the man. She knew his presence here was meant to intimidate her.

"I came to see if there's anything you need."

"I need you to step back and respect my personal space." Cassidy's hand went to her holster, and she slipped the leather strap back in case she needed to draw her weapon.

Gilead raised his hands and did as she asked. He didn't look offended in the least. No, if anything, he looked amused. "Of course. I didn't realize you had space issues."

"I don't. You do."

The side of his lip curled. "You know, I think we've got chemistry."

"I think you're delusional."

He leaned against the wall and crossed his arms. "You know, God gave me a vision about you."

"Funny. He didn't give me any visions about you." Cassidy's words sounded lighthearted, but in reality

Gilead's statement had made her insides turn ice cold. She wasn't really sure she wanted to hear what he had to say and feared he had the upper-hand as he played these mental games with her.

Gilead either didn't hear her or didn't bother to acknowledge what she'd said. "In my vision, we formed a great team."

"I'll never be on your side."

"You might change your mind. I can help you, Cassidy." The look in Gilead's eyes almost looked sincere and genuine. His gentle demeanor was offset by the startling truth about what Cassidy knew about him —that the man was a monster.

Though her first instinct was to rebuke him, Cassidy decided on a different plan. She would play along for a moment. She needed to know what he was thinking, and this might be one of the only ways of finding out.

"Help me with what?" Cassidy asked, the words feeling acidic in her throat.

"I can help you heal the hurts you're carrying around."

Sweat trickled down her back as Gilead's presence began to overwhelm her. As she felt like he was touching her without actually doing so. As she felt like she couldn't get her breath. "I don't know what you're talking about."

He inched closer, the motion so seamless that she almost didn't notice. Cassidy should tell him to back off, but she was too focused on what he might say next.

Was he the one who'd sent her that text? This could be her moment to find out all the information she needed to know.

"I think you do." Gilead's voice was so low it was barely audible, and his eyes bore into hers.

"You're wrong."

"You've never been loved for who you are, have you? It's only been for what you can do for other people. What you can offer. That's why you take your job as police chief so seriously. If you help people, they'll love you in return and you'll feel like you belong."

Cassidy's throat tightened. She wanted to deny Gilead's words. But what if he was right?

"You want to help people, but you constantly feel like you've let them down. You try not to live with a performance-based standard, but you do. Your worthiness is based on how well you do. I'm guessing this is because of your upbringing."

Some of the blood drained from Cassidy's face, and her lungs tightened as anxiety reared in her. "You don't know what you're talking about."

Gilead continued, almost as if he didn't hear her. "You love your husband, but you're uncertain about your future. You're not sure what it's going to hold for the both of you."

"You're just guessing," Cassidy said. "My future with Ty is very certain."

Gilead had inched close enough that Cassidy could

see the flecks of gold in his gaze. There was nowhere for her to go. She was trapped there in the corner of the kitchen with Gilead in front of her.

She wanted to run. To flee. To pull her gun.

But Cassidy forced herself to remain still and to finish this conversation.

"I want you to be a part of us here at Gilead's Cove, Cassidy." Gilead's calm words washed over her. "I want you to realize your full potential—as a person. For what's inside of you. Not what you can do for other people."

"How would I do that here?" The words burned as they left her throat. They sounded earnest—so earnest, Cassidy almost had herself tricked.

No, his words weren't true and Cassidy didn't believe them. She was simply playing along so she could try to get information.

Gilead reached forward until he touched her arm, his eyes nearly hypnotizing and his hand feeling like fire. "I could teach you, Cassidy. Me personally. It's what God is telling me to do. He wants me to help you make your life better."

The door squeaked open behind them, and Cassidy nearly jumped out of her skin.

As Gilead stepped back, her gaze jerked toward the space. A man she'd never seen before stepped inside.

"I just wanted to make sure you didn't need anything," he said, looking at Gilead like a foot soldier ready to do whatever bidding he was asked to do.

Gilead scowled, as if he didn't appreciate the interruption. "We're fine. Thank you, Enoch."

Cassidy released her breath and squeezed past Gilead. She was done. The moment was broken, and she wouldn't get any more from the man. Besides, she didn't think she could handle any more of that conversation. Her skin was already crawling.

"I think I'm good here," she said. "I'll find Ty and be going. Thank you for your cooperation."

It wasn't until Cassidy stepped outside that she felt like she could finally breathe again.

But her relief was short-lived when she saw Moriah standing near the door of the RV. The woman's gaze was focused on Cassidy, and her eyes were narrowed in a death glare.

———

TY GLANCED around the compound as he walked, keeping an eye open for Serena. Where was the girl? It was almost as if an alarm had sounded here at Gilead's Cove, sending everyone back to their trailers. Not a soul was outside.

"The only other place Barnabas would have left anything would be here." Kaleb opened the door to the Meeting Place.

Ty stepped inside and surveyed the space. Again, no one was visible, almost like this place had become a ghost town.

"Anywhere in particular in here where Barnabas may have left something?"

Kaleb nodded toward a hallway across the massive room with a wooden stage and rows of chairs. "He kept some of the electronics he used at the front gate in there. He was a construction worker by trade, but he knew quite a bit about technology. I guess before he came here, one of his specialties was wiring home entertainment systems."

Ty opened the door to the closet and a jumble of wires and plastic boxes stared back at him. He shuffled through several things but saw nothing that gave him any clues.

How did this all tie in together?

"You all heard from Lela lately?" Kaleb asked quietly from behind him.

Ty shrugged. "Not to my knowledge."

"Do you know if she's . . . safe?"

Ty glanced back, surprised by the change in conversation. The man had been tight-lipped on the walk here. "She is safe. You sound worried."

Kaleb's demeanor remained stoic, but concern flickered in his gaze. "I just think about her a lot."

Ty turned back to the closet as he searched for any type of clue that could help them with this case. "I'm sure Cassidy would be happy to find out something about her . . . if you'd be willing to help her out as well."

"I have nothing to say." Kaleb's voice hardened again.

After a few minutes of searching, Ty sighed and straightened. There was nothing here.

"Thanks for letting me look," Ty said. "I'd like to go back to Cassidy now, though."

"Of course."

They started walking back toward the trailer.

"I didn't know Barnabas had any drugs here, just so you know," Kaleb offered, shoving his hands down deep into his pockets as a contemplative expression crossed his face. "Those drugs that were found in my brother's car several weeks ago truly were my brother's drugs."

"You think Barnabas had a side business going on?" Ty asked, glancing around the trailers around him.

It still looked like a ghost town, and there was no sign of Serena. The whole thing was eerie, reminding Ty of some kind of drill residents were doing to keep quiet.

"I suppose it's a possibility," Kaleb said. "Though we do monitor our residents here and expect them to adhere to certain standards, if someone was desperate enough, they could hide things from us. Barnabas was one of Gilead's trusted men. He had special privileges that allowed him more freedom than others."

"How do certain people get more of these 'freedoms'?"

"Gilead tests certain ones for loyalty," Kaleb said.

"What kind of tests?" Ty didn't like the sound of that.

Kaleb shrugged. "It's complicated."

As much as Ty wanted to ask more questions about these tests, he was nearly back to the trailer where he'd left Cassidy, and he had other questions for Kaleb before their time ran out.

"Do you know where Serena is?" Ty asked.

Kaleb cast a quick glance his way. "Serena? Are you still worried about her? I've already spoken to Cassidy on the phone about her."

"She's our friend, and we're concerned about her."

Kaleb shrugged, like it wasn't a big deal. "She actually seems very happy here."

"But is she safe?" Irritation edged into Ty's voice. Serena was the type who could be happy doing a lot of things. It wasn't her happiness that concerned Ty. It was her well-being.

"We're not monsters, you know."

Ty wasn't so sure about that. "It's not most of you I'm worried about. It's Gilead."

Just as Ty said the words, he spotted Cassidy. She looked pale as she stood outside the trailer. Another woman—was that Moriah?—walked away.

Ty glanced behind Cassidy just in time to see Gilead leave the very trailer where Cassidy had been working.

His hands fisted. What had that man been doing in there? His stomach churned at the thought that Gilead had been near Cassidy.

"Good afternoon, Ty." Gilead stopped near him.

Ty didn't reply, only glowered at him.

"I'll go and let you two finish up here," Gilead continued. "Hope you find what you're looking for."

As he walked away, his words echoed in Ty's mind.

Hope you find what you're looking for.

What was it about that phrase that triggered something in him? Buried memories fought to break out and come alive in his mind.

He'd have to think about them later. Right now, he had to know if Cassidy was okay.

CHAPTER TWENTY-THREE

"WHAT HAPPENED BACK THERE?" Ty asked.

Cassidy gripped the steering wheel, still mentally replaying the whole conversation herself as they drove away from Gilead's Cove. "I don't even know."

"What do you mean you don't know?"

She raked a hand through her hair. "Ty, it was like Gilead had some kind of mind control over me. I started thinking that I'd play along and just see what kind of information he might offer."

"But . . ."

"But . . . some of the things he said were spot-on. It was like he could see inside me."

"He's just good at reading people."

"I agree that he's good at reading people. Or maybe he does know about my background."

"How would he have found out?"

"If someone got nosy enough, they could find out.

You and I both know that. That's why my goal has been to stay under the radar. To keep my face off the news and out of the newspaper."

Ty studied her a moment. "There's more, isn't there?"

"I just can't shake the feeling that he was somehow hypnotizing me. I know it sounds crazy." Cassidy shook her head, trying to shake away the thoughts. "But what I started out faking turned into a real curiosity."

Ty straightened, and something close to anger flashed in his gaze. "I don't like that man."

"I don't either." Cassidy glanced at Ty. "I guess you didn't see Serena?"

"No sign of her. I did ask Kaleb about her. He said she seems happy."

"That doesn't really mean much." Cassidy let out a long sigh.

"I know. Kaleb is still worried about his sister. You might be able to use that as leverage if push comes to shove."

"Maybe." Cassidy's voice still sounded heavy, even to her own ears. The reality of just how influential Gilead was crushed down on her. She'd thought she was stronger than to fall under his spell. But, for just a moment, she'd believed his words.

The other part of their conversation came to her mind. The part about them being together.

Should she tell Ty that? It would just make him hate

the man even more. Yet she didn't want to keep secrets from him.

She opened her mouth to speak when her phone rang. It was Clemson.

"Can you come down to the clinic?" he asked.

"Is this about Bob?"

"It sure is."

"I'll be right there."

That conversation would have to wait.

———

CASSIDY DROPPED Ty off before heading to the island's small clinic. She waved hello to the receptionist as she passed and went straight back to Doc Clemson's office. He was sitting at his desk staring at a file when she knocked on his open door.

Clemson pushed his wire-framed glasses up higher on his nose. "Cassidy. Thanks for coming. Have a seat."

"You couldn't keep me away." She lowered herself into an upholstered chair across from her friend and waited for his news.

Clemson drew in a deep breath and laced hands together atop his desk. "I sent off the samples from the autopsy and marked them urgent," he started. "Any time it's a city official, we have to consider that the death might be suspicious."

"Agreed."

"Initially, it looked like Bob died of a heart attack.

But, as I told you earlier, I was Bob's doctor, and he would have told me if he'd been having any problems that were out of the ordinary."

Cassidy wondered exactly where this was going, but she waited patiently for Clemson to continue.

"Anyway, I got the report back surprisingly early," Doc Clemson said. "And I thought you would want to know right away what I discovered."

"I'm dying here, Doc. I need information." He was drawing this out way too long for her taste.

He shoved a paper toward her. "To sum it up, we found traces of Nerium and Bisacodyl."

The words sounded vaguely familiar to Cassidy, but she needed more information and she needed it more quickly than her recollections allowed at the moment. "I'm going to need the plain-speak version, Doc."

Clemson frowned. "Oleander and a stimulant laxative."

Cassidy tilted her head as she processed his words. "I've heard of people being poisoned by oleander, but I've never actually known it to happen."

"Me neither. It's fascinating, really. Oleander by itself could cause heart problems, but when combined with the stimulant laxative, there would definitely be a reaction that mimics a heart attack. It could be practically undetectable if someone wasn't looking hard enough."

"Did someone mix them together on purpose? Did

they come up with this fatal mix just for the purpose of trying to stump police?"

Clemson nodded slowly, his intelligent gaze flickering with interest. "That's what I suspect. Oleander sap may have been boiled into a liquid and then the laxative added. It was probably mixed into a drink that has a strong flavor. Whoever drank it was probably clueless as to what was in their cup."

Cassidy drew in a few breaths before voicing her final thought. "So Bob didn't die of natural causes. This was first degree murder."

Clemson nodded with a frown. "That's correct."

"Thank you for the update." Cassidy stood. She needed to call Abbott because she wondered if their other victims had died the same death.

It was a possibility definitely worth exploring.

CHAPTER TWENTY-FOUR

BACK AT HER OFFICE, Cassidy called Abbott with the update, and he promised to put a rush on having the other bodies tested for oleander and a stimulate laxative as well. She felt certain they'd find similar results.

In the meantime, Cassidy also sent a sample of the flakka to the state lab. She needed to confirm what the drug was and what strain it might be, since different gangs had different signatures they put on the substance.

At least she was inching closer to answers.

She leaned back in her chair and thought things through again.

What if Barnabas was selling these drugs? What if he used Reagan to help him with that?

And the stuffed animals . . . could they have planted the drugs inside the toys in order to go undetected?

Cassidy thought it was a good theory.

And that led her also to wonder about the three bodies they'd found. If Reagan was connected to Barnabas and to the flakka, why had she died? Had she become too much of a liability?

It seemed plausible.

That could also explain who those men were on the boat. What if they were connected to Barnabas and trying to protect their secret?

She needed to figure out a way to confirm this.

And there was only one person who came to mind.

Jimmy James.

Jimmy James reminded Cassidy of a mix of Popeye and Brutus. He worked down at the docks and had huge muscles and a stocky build. Though he looked rough on the outside, he was a good guy at heart. He also seemed to have a finger on the pulse of crime in the area.

Cassidy decided to pay him a visit. He had been a good informant in the past.

She pulled up at the docks fifteen minutes later, parked, and began walking along the boardwalk there. The scent of the sea wafted with the breeze—a mix of salty air, fish, and eel grass. The area was mostly empty, but several large boats that were kept at the area year-round floated in the slips.

A huge fishing center sat at the entrance to the property, a place where people could sign up for charter boat tours, buy supplies from drinks to tackle, or browse accessories for their boats.

Six boats down, Cassidy spotted the man in the glowing orange of the sinking sun. He was hard to miss.

Jimmy James stopped cleaning a boat for long enough to look up and smile. "Chief Chambers, what brings you here? You looking to charter a fishing trip?"

"Not quite. I was hoping you had time for a question or two."

"Sure thing." He put the water hose down and turned to her. "What's up?"

Cassidy glanced around. No one else was close enough to hear. "Listen, I'm looking for two men on a skiff."

"That could be a lot of people, Chief." Jimmy James almost sounded apologetic as he said the words.

"I know. But I just saw them two days ago. They wore all black. Had guns."

His face paled, and he crossed his bulky arms. "Sounds like trouble, Chief. You know I'm trying to stay away from people like that."

He knew something, Cassidy realized. She just had to get him to open up. She knew he feared getting in trouble with the law, and she needed to put him at ease.

"I know you are, Jimmy James," she started. "But I also know you're an excellent watchman. Between you and me, I'm afraid these men may be guilty of killing more than one person, and I need to find them. Desperately. Is there anything you can think of to help me? Anything at all?"

He shifted, as if uneasy. His gaze scanned the docks around them before he turned back to her. "We don't have as many boats going out at this time of year as we do in the summer, of course."

"I know this was just a small boat," Cassidy said. "I couldn't get the exact make of it. And I know boats that small aren't even launched here, necessarily. It could have come over from Ocracoke or the Mainland."

He frowned, and his muscles flexed as he glanced around again. "You said these guys might have killed some people?"

"That's right. They're suspects in a murder investigation."

He let out a breath, his gaze heavy as he looked at Cassidy. "You know I could get in a lot of trouble if people found out I was a blabbermouth."

"That's why it doesn't have to go past me. This is a conversation between you and me. No one else has to know." Cassidy's voice was unwavering. She meant the words.

He still hesitated and glanced around. "People are going to see me talking to you."

"What do you suggest?"

He nodded behind him. "We can use this boat. No one will see us there."

A moment of hesitation rose in Cassidy. Though she mostly trusted Jimmy James, she still knew the man had a dangerous side. Would she be safe in there with him alone?

She prayed the answer was yes. He'd never tried to harm her before.

"Okay." She stepped onto the yacht, Jimmy James behind her. He directed her into the cabin, glanced around, and shut the door before turning back toward her again.

"I might know who you're talking about," he started.

"This is important," Cassidy prodded, sensing he was still hesitant. "Anything will help."

"These two guys have been down at the docks. They look like trouble. I can smell it a mile away, to be honest."

It was too bad Jimmy James had such a bad rap sheet because he'd make a good cop otherwise. The man was observant. "You ever see them before?"

"Yeah, I seen them on and off. Like you said, they mostly wear black. Have shifty eyes. But it wasn't my business, right?"

Her pulse spiked with anticipation. "What do you know about them?"

"Not much. And I might not have noticed them at all. But I saw them loading up a boat once, and some of their cargo caught my eye."

"Why's that?"

"Because they had a box full of stuffed animals."

———

CASSIDY FELT something ignite inside her. Stuffed animals? This had to be the link she'd been searching for.

"Can you describe these guys?"

He shrugged. "Not really. I think they were in their twenties or thirties. White guys. On the thin side."

"But you couldn't identify them if you saw a picture?"

He shrugged again. "I can't say for sure. But I can tell you that they went into the shop to buy some supplies last time."

"Are there security cameras inside?"

"You know it. I can see what I can find out—as long as you keep my name out of this."

"A promise is a promise."

Jimmy James paused and shook his head. "Chief, I know you know this. But these guys didn't look like the type to play games. Are you sure you don't want to let this go?"

"I can't let this go, Jimmy James. Not only is it my sworn duty, but these guys are dangerous. They shouldn't get away with murder."

"I'll see what I can find out then."

"Thank you. I appreciate it."

She opened the door, ready to go back to the station armed with this new information. Just as she stepped onto the deck, something skipped across the metal, sounding like an acorn on a fall day.

But it wasn't an acorn.

Before she could react, the world around her exploded.

CHAPTER TWENTY-FIVE

CASSIDY HIT THE WATER. The icy cold liquid caused her lungs to instantly freeze. Her mind froze too—just for a moment—along with the world around her.

Air, she realized. She needed air.

She forced her eyes open. The water stung them, begging her to close them again, but she couldn't.

Tiny fireballs cut through the water around her.

The boat. It had exploded.

Someone had thrown . . . a grenade onboard?

Those men. It had to have been those men.

Just then, another thought hit her. Jimmy James?

Where was he?

Eyes still open in the murky water, Cassidy rotated in the liquid world around her. Jimmy James wasn't within her sight. She could only see shards of the boat littering the water.

Her lungs squeezed tighter. Cassidy had to make it to the surface, she realized. She wouldn't survive down here much longer without any air.

But what if the person who did this was still there? Was still up above the surface, watching to see if their plan had worked?

Making a quick decision, Cassidy swam beneath the dock to the other side. A dark shadow floated above her.

Another boat, she realized.

She crossed underneath it before bursting through the water.

As her head bobbed above the surface, she sucked in a deep breath. Her greedy lungs hungrily gulped in air. Her chest heaved with exertion.

She swung her head back toward the open water in the distance.

A boat pulled away.

It looked like the same boat with the men who'd shot at Cassidy and her crew earlier.

They had done this.

But what about Jimmy James?

"Chief, is that you?" someone said from the boardwalk. "Are you okay?"

She glanced back and saw two men. They knelt on the ground, reaching for her.

Tate Donovan, she remembered. And Ryan Something.

They were both volunteers with the local rescue squad.

Cassidy reached for their outstretched hands. She didn't think she could drag herself out of the water on her own strength. Her muscles felt like Jell-O.

Tate pulled her onto the boardwalk, and she clung to the ground, waiting for her world to right itself. She gasped for air, trying to get her energy back—and to remember everything that had to be done.

Her gaze jerked toward the yacht. At least, to the area where the yacht had been.

Only the bow was visible now—the rest of the boat sank beneath the water or had been blown into shreds.

"Jimmy James." Her teeth chattered as she pointed toward the wreckage.

Ryan took off toward the boat. Cassidy wanted to go herself. But her muscles had frozen with the cold, and her energy evaporated like saltwater on a hot day.

A moment later, a blanket was draped over her shoulders. Cassidy muttered thanks and watched as Ryan dove into the water.

What kind of men carried around grenades?

Dangerous ones.

Had those men on the boat known Cassidy would be here? She didn't think so. No one knew.

They must have seen her and been prepared . . .

The thought wasn't comforting.

"You need . . . to call . . . backup," she said.

Tate knelt beside her. "I already did. You need to be checked out as well."

"I'm fine."

"Doc Clemson might feel otherwise."

Cassidy looked up for a better view of the dark-haired man and offered a grateful smile. "Thank you for your help."

"Of course. I just happened to be walking outside when I saw the explosion. I'm on the volunteer rescue squad, but during the day I run the books for the fishing center."

"Thank goodness you were near," Cassidy said.

As the words left her lips, someone emerged from the water.

Cassidy stood for a better look.

No, that was two people.

Ryan . . . and Jimmy James.

He was okay.

Thank God, he was okay.

But that had been too close for comfort.

———

"ARE YOU SURE YOU'RE OKAY?" Ty asked Cassidy again, studying her face for any sign she was in pain that she refused to admit.

They sat in Tate's office at the fishing center, and Cassidy had changed into some yoga pants and a sweatshirt Ty had brought her. Her wet hair had been pulled back into a bun, and Cassidy had recovered enough from her scare to snap back into work mode.

"I'm fine. I promise."

She'd called Ty and told him what happened. He'd shown up at the docks only fifteen minutes later, desperate to see with his own eyes that Cassidy was indeed okay.

That had been close, Ty mused. Too close. If Cassidy hadn't stepped out the cabin door on the yacht when she did and been thrown into the water, she might be dead right now. Ty could hardly stomach the thought.

Jimmy James had been taken to a hospital in Raleigh. Paramedics thought he may have broken some ribs and suffered a concussion. But he should be okay —thankfully.

Meanwhile, Abbott and his team arrived on the scene to take over.

"So you think it was a grenade?" Ty asked Cassidy, still trying to get a better picture about what had happened.

She took a sip of her coffee. "It's the only thing that makes sense."

"Do you think these guys were watching you?"

Cassidy let out a long breath. "No, not really. Honestly, I'd guess that maybe they were coming in for the day and spotted me with Jimmy James. Maybe they just put things together and decided to eliminate the problem."

Ty frowned. "This all sounds extreme. The fact they

had a grenade? Normal people don't carry one around. And what if these are the guys who poisoned those other people?"

Cassidy held her coffee closer, the steam from the cup rising to meet her face. "I'm not so sure these are the guys who poisoned them. My guess is that Barnabas was behind the poisoning. These guys are connected with the drugs."

It sounded like a twisted web—one they needed to quickly unravel. "Hopefully the Coast Guard or marine police will catch them."

"Hopefully. But these guys had a head start. Too much of a head start, if you ask me." Just as Cassidy said the words, the door opened, and Tate Donovan stepped inside.

Ty had met him once while out fishing with Austin, and the man seemed like a nice enough addition to the island—even if he did scream more big city charm than small island beach bum.

"How are you feeling?" he asked Cassidy. "Are you sure I can't take you to the clinic?"

"I'm fine. The worst thing is the ringing in my ears. But otherwise, I just have a few scratches."

He stood a few feet away, hands on his hips, and nodded. "I'm glad to hear that. This could have been much worse."

Cassidy turned toward him. "Listen, I need to scroll through some video from a couple days ago. Do you have access to that? You said you worked here in the office, correct?"

"That's right. I do books. I'd be happy to see what we have. I think we keep five days' worth of security footage on file before our program starts to record over it. Video takes up so much space on a hard drive."

"So I've heard." Cassidy followed Tate down the hallway, motioning for Ty to come along also.

He set them up in a little room and showed them how to find what they were looking for. And then he left them on their own.

Ty watched Cassidy scroll through the feed but said nothing. He knew she needed space to process things.

"This all happened because Jimmy James was talking with me," Cassidy muttered. "Those guys must have seen us and gotten scared. Jimmy James said he thought he'd seen the men here before. So these guys should be on the security footage. Jimmy James saw them come in to purchase some supplies."

"They came in that day? The same day they fired on you?" Ty asked.

"That's my impression. At least it narrows down a time." She continued to scroll until she reached Wednesday morning. She backed the video up until she reached the time the store opened at eight and then hit play.

They watched as some families came in. A single guy. A group of older men.

No one that seemed to match the description.

"They fired those shots at around ten," Cassidy said. "We're running out of time here."

"Let's not give up hope yet." Ty draped his arm around the back of the chair, at times wishing she had a safer profession where she wasn't constantly in the line of fire.

The truth remained that he could have lost her today. Easily. Too easily.

A surge of protectiveness rose in him. He'd almost lost her more than once already. He would do everything in his power not to let that happen again.

"Whoa, look at this." Cassidy leaned closer to the screen. "Two men in black. I think these could be our guys."

Ty leaned closer also and examined the men. He didn't recognize them. Granted, the images weren't the clearest. But it did, at least, give them an idea of what these guys looked like.

"Any idea who they are?" Ty asked.

Cassidy squinted. "You know, this one looks vaguely familiar, but the image isn't clear enough for me to make out his features."

"It's a start, right?"

"Absolutely. I've got to get copies of this and send the video to area police departments. I need to know if anyone else recognizes them." Cassidy's gaze locked with his. "Ty, if these guys were here at the docks today, then there's a good chance they're staying somewhere on this island. And based on their actions, they're guilty. I've got to find them."

"Thankfully, you have a lot of help. Don't forget that you don't have to do everything on your own."

"I won't." She squeezed his hand. "I promise that I won't."

CHAPTER TWENTY-SIX

ON A WHIM, Cassidy paid a man named Davy White a visit.

She went to church with Davy, and the man had the only exterminating and landscaping business on the island. She knew it was a long shot, but he was one of the few people on Lantern Beach who might be able to answer the questions she had.

With Ty by her side, and freshly showered and changed, she knocked at Davy's door. His wife answered and offered a warm smile when she spotted them. "Ty, Cassidy. What a surprise."

"Hi, Sue," Cassidy said. "I have a question for your husband about a case I'm working. Is he available?"

"Is he in trouble?" Sue's voice caught, and she clutched the door knob.

"Not at all," Cassidy murmured, trying to put her at ease. "I'm hoping he can help me, actually."

Sue nodded and took a step back. "Let me get him then."

Davy, a short and stocky man with prickly hair all over his face and the top of his head, appeared a few minutes later.

"I hear you need my help?" he started, wiping some crumbs from his shirt.

"Do you have a minute?" Cassidy asked.

"Of course. Come on in. We just finished dinner."

A few minutes later they were seated across from him on a floral couch in the living room. Sue had brought them lemonade and made herself scarce.

"I used to want to be a police officer when I was younger, you know," Davy said, tugging at his pant legs.

"What happened?" Ty asked, slipping his arm across the back of the couch.

"I was robbed at gunpoint once, and after that I realized I was a scaredy cat."

"I don't know," Cassidy said. "You deal with bugs and rodents. They scare me."

Davy laughed. "Well, I guess we all have our thing then, don't we?"

"I guess we do." Cassidy shifted and set her drink down. "Listen, I'm looking for a particular plant that might be found here on the island. I was hoping that maybe you'd seen something since your company does extermination work as well as lawn care."

"Any way I can help."

Cassidy showed him a picture on her phone. "This is the plant."

He took the device from her, glanced at the picture, and nodded nonchalantly. "That's oleander."

A moment of victory washed over her, and she shared a glance with Ty.

"Yes, exactly," she muttered.

Davy gave her phone back. "There's only one place I've ever seen that plant here on the island."

"Where is that, Davy?"

"Margie Witherspoon's old residence. She used to love gardening. She passed away five years ago, and someone else purchased her house. Now they do long-term rentals. Of course, renters haven't kept up with the garden."

Cassidy's breath hitched. "What's the address, Davy?"

He gave it to them.

Cassidy knew exactly where she needed to head. The answers were so close, she could practically reach out and touch them.

NO ONE ANSWERED the door at the little cottage located at 23194 Wilmington Drive.

But someone *had* been there recently. The trash can was full of discarded food that still smelled fresh. That meant the resident couldn't be but so far away.

Cassidy and Ty headed over to the next-door neighbor's house and pounded on the door, hoping to get some information from whoever lived here. A man in a tank top and pajama bottoms answered the door and scowled at Cassidy—until he saw her police uniform.

"Can I help you?" He held a ukulele, and his fingers brushed across the strings as he lowered his hands.

"I have a question about the house next door," she started.

"Sure. I'm Walt. What do you need?" He pushed the instrument behind his back and turned his full attention on Cassidy and Ty. "I've been using YouTube videos to learn to play the ukulele. Thankfully, there's a pause button."

"Best of luck with that," Cassidy said. "I was wondering if you'd met the person who's staying beside you?"

"Yeah, I sure have. A man named James Waldron, I believe." The man rolled his eyes. "He was a piece of work."

Finally, Cassidy had a name. Nothing delighted her more than progress. "Why do you say this Waldron guy was a piece of work? What do you know about him?"

"He worked for the ferry system, I believe."

The ferry system? Wait. That's where Cassidy had seen the man before. He was the one who'd met Cassidy when she'd gone to talk to Rodgers. The man had been a watchdog—for more than one reason, it appeared.

"Seemed like a respectable enough job," Walt continued, his arms flying out as he gestured to emphasize every other word. "But that guy was as unfriendly as they come. He never said anything to anyone. The one time I tried to talk to him, he gave me the bird and kept walking."

"Sounds like he won't win any awards for congeniality," Cassidy said.

Walt snorted. "No, he won't. He just looked mean."

"You ever see anyone with him?"

"Not really. Well, I take that back. There was one guy that I saw over there a couple times."

Cassidy's breath caught. Maybe they were finally on to something. "You remember anything about him?"

"Not much. Like I said, he didn't want to chat. He came and went a lot."

"Did he have a boat?" Ty asked.

Walt nodded. "Yeah, he did. It was parked in the driveway for a while but disappeared a few weeks ago. I assumed he'd launched it. If you cut through the woods there, it leads to the water. I'm pretty sure he was docking it there, though I don't know why anyone would want to go tromping through that tick-infested area."

Cassidy and Ty exchanged a glance.

"That's very helpful," Cassidy said. "When was the last time you saw Waldron?"

"Yesterday morning. He hasn't been home since then."

Cassidy took a step back, satisfied with this new information. "You're sure?"

"I'm sure. It's always a relief when he's not there. I don't feel like he's watching me and scowling."

"Understood. Thanks for your help, Walt."

He pulled his ukulele back around and strummed it a moment. "Oh, and there's one more thing. He had this weird fascination with stuffed animals. I only know because I saw him carrying a large bag and one dropped out. What kind of man carries a bagful of stuffed animals through the woods?"

Cassidy glanced at Ty again. She knew exactly what kind of person did that.

The drug-dealing, gun-toting, grenade-throwing type.

———

CASSIDY CALLED in Leggott and Dane to search James Waldron's place. Before she'd left the scene, she'd found the oleander bush. Not only had she found it, but it appeared several branches had been recently clipped.

This was their guy. She felt certain of it.

Ty remained by her side as Cassidy went back to her office at police headquarters. She was going to find out everything she could about James Waldron. She typed his name into a search engine, and pages of results popped up.

"Look at that," Cassidy muttered. "He really does work for the ferry system."

"And it looks like he only moved to the island six months ago to take the job," Ty said. "I have no doubt he's our guy."

"I need to call his boss and see what he has to say."

Cassidy called Rodgers, who told her that Waldron had called in sick for the past two days. He also said he had no reason to suspect that the man was doing anything illegal, that he was rough around the edges but he'd been a good worker.

Cassidy managed to obtain Waldron's cell phone number from Rodgers, but when she tried to trace it, the device didn't ping. Waldron had most likely turned it off or discarded it.

This was her guy. This was one of the men who'd most likely shot at her, who'd thrown that grenade at her, and who was involved in these other deaths.

"What else did you find out about him?" Ty asked, staring at the computer screen.

Cassidy leaned closer. "Let's see. He was in the army for four years."

"That could explain the grenade."

Everything seemed to be falling in place—every-thing except his current location. "True. And since Waldron worked for the ferry system, he would know these waterways. He may have been keeping an eye on that area by the lighthouse. He'd also know when and where he could do his drug deals without being caught.

Maybe he even transported certain items onto the ferry while he was on the job. No one would have thought twice about it."

"You're probably right. And being on the ferry, he would hear all the town scuttlebutt."

Cassidy sucked in a deep breath. "Ty, I saw some stuffed animals being collected at the ferry docks. Do you think . . ."

"That it could be a cover for drug smuggling? I think it's a very good possibility."

Cassidy stared at Waldron's picture. Stared at his eyes.

It was like the neighbor had said— Waldron had a mean look to his gaze. His hair was longish, his lip slightly curled in a smile that showed he was up to something, and he had tattoos on his forearms.

Cassidy put out a call to the officers on the island as well as to the NCSBI. Hopefully between everyone, someone would see something and report back. In the meantime, she would go to the docks and check out those stuffed animals herself.

They were close to closing in on these guys—so close that Cassidy could almost taste victory.

CHAPTER TWENTY-SEVEN

MORIAH GRIPPED the bouquet of wildflowers in her hands and glanced around. Rows of people stood from their chairs in the Meeting Place, each person staring at her as one of the members of Gilead's Cove played a soft melody on a flute.

She'd never felt more beautiful than she did right now in her simple white dress with her long hair full of soft curls and her rose-scented skin.

This was it. This was her big day. The moment her life would change forever.

And nothing would ruin it.

Her hands trembled as she spotted Gilead. He stood at the end of the aisle dressed in a suit and looking more handsome than ever. His bright smile was all she needed to see—for now and forever.

As she reached the stage, Gilead took her hands. He leaned closer.

"You look beautiful," he murmured.

Her cheeks warmed at his attention. "Thank you."

The rest of the ceremony was a blur of absolute elation.

Moriah Roberts became Mrs. Anthony Gilead.

Now Gilead's kingdom here would become her own. She couldn't wait for the transition, for the progression.

After the ceremony, everyone gathered for a party. Gone was the dour look on people's faces as they ate their normally rationed foods. A feast had been prepared, and Moriah was the center of attention. No one would dare look down on her now.

She'd forgotten how much she liked to be the center of attention, back before the world had worn her down. But with each pat on her back, with each look of envy, with every glance of jealousy other women gave her, something began to grow bigger and bigger inside her.

Pride, she realized. She was getting her pride and self-esteem back. It felt wonderful.

As she talked to a few of the ladies, Gilead appeared by her side. He leaned closer, his breath tickling her ear.

"I'll be right back," Gilead whispered.

"I'll be waiting."

She talked for a few more minutes when a new thought hit her.

Their marriage license.

They hadn't gotten one.

And Moriah hadn't signed anything.

She wondered if Gilead had somehow overlooked that. Maybe in the rush of everything, the formality had slipped his mind.

She should mention it to him before she forgot also. Though they'd had a ceremony, they had to make this union official.

Quietly, she slipped away and walked upstairs. She paused as she heard voices drifting out from Gilead's office.

She peered through the doorway. Her husband spoke with two men she'd never seen before. Who were they? And why were they here right now of all times?

Their words caught her ear.

"We need to find a way to get to her alone," one of the men said.

"I don't know what to tell you," Gilead responded. "This isn't my job."

"She knows too much," the other man said. "She could bring us all down. Not just us. You too."

"Like I said, this isn't my problem." Gilead's voice rose in a way Moriah had never heard it before. "Now you need to take care of this issue. And the sooner the better. You obviously botched things yesterday and the time before that as well. There better not be any trails leading the authorities back here."

"There aren't," the first man said.

"Good," Gilead remarked. "Now take care of Cassidy Chambers."

"Yes, sir."

Cassidy Chambers? Moriah sucked in a deep breath. Why was Gilead talking about the police chief?

She still remembered the shock she'd felt yesterday when she'd caught Gilead and Cassidy in the RV together. Cassidy had even looked flushed as she'd stepped out.

Just what had they been doing in that trailer? Was the woman trying to steal Gilead from her? Had she lured him there? In fact, maybe that was why Cassidy had warned her not to marry Gilead—it was because she wanted him herself.

A new surge of anger rose inside her.

That was unacceptable.

As she heard footsteps, she backed into her old room and ducked behind the door.

She watched as Gilead emerged and straightened his suit before heading down the stairs.

When his footsteps had disappeared, his two friends stepped out.

Feeling impulsive, Moriah stepped out and stopped them.

"You want to get Cassidy Chambers alone?" she whispered.

"We do," one man said.

"I know just the way to do it. I can help."

They glanced at each other, as if uncertain.

"You don't have to do that," the scarier of the two men said.

He definitely wasn't the type she'd want to meet in a

dark alley. No, he wasn't the type anyone wanted to meet.

Which made him perfect.

Moriah smiled "I want to help. Believe me, I want to."

CHAPTER TWENTY-EIGHT

CASSIDY SIGHED AND STEPPED BACK. "Oh, Lisa. You look so beautiful."

Her friend had tried on her wedding dress, even though the ceremony was still four hours away. A photographer was going to take some photos before the ceremony, and the weather had turned out perfect.

Cassidy desperately wanted the day to remain perfect. She'd even tried to delegate her work so that could happen.

Including the fiasco with the stuffed animals at the dock. She'd gone there last night, and, sure enough, she'd found drugs hidden in the animals. Rodgers had told her that it had been Waldron's idea to collect the toys. When they'd looked into the nonprofit they were being donated to, they'd found out it didn't exist.

She still had a lot more work to do. But, for now, she

had to trust that her people were doing their jobs. That Abbott was dependable and trustworthy.

Because Cassidy wouldn't miss her friend's wedding for anything.

Lisa looked in the full-length mirror in the room located above her restaurant and glowed. "Thank you. I can't believe the big day is finally here."

"Well, I saw Braden earlier, and he might as well have swallowed a light bulb. I don't think I've ever seen him look so happy." Cassidy paused. "Although, I have to say, I was surprised you let him go over to Hatteras with Ty."

"Well, I can't believe our rings weren't finished being sized by the jeweler until this morning. I feel like they're kind of important for the ceremony."

"I concur. And the guys still have plenty of time to get back from Hatteras with them. You should be good."

"I still pinch myself that I actually met Braden." Lisa smiled back at Cassidy. "I mean, we've had our ups and downs, but I can't imagine my life without him."

"I know the feeling, and I'm so happy for you two." Cassidy grinned. "This is going to be a great day."

"And I'm so happy that you survived that boat explosion yesterday and can be at my wedding." Lisa gave her a motherly look. "You've got to stop getting in these life-threatening situations."

"Believe me, I know." Cassidy's entire body hurt

this morning, but she wouldn't tell Lisa that. No, she didn't want anything to ruin her friend's day.

Someone knocked at the door, and Skye stepped inside. The light still hadn't returned to her eyes. Cassidy knew she was still worried about her niece—and she would be until Serena was away from Gilead's Cove. Her heart pounded with compassion for her friend.

"I couldn't miss all the fun," Skye said, attempting a smile. "Your BFF only gets married once."

"I seriously can't believe this is the day!" Lisa squealed, fluffing her skirt and twirling around.

Cassidy's phone rang, and she excused herself. Though she didn't recognize the number, she answered anyway. "Cassidy Chambers."

"Cassidy?" a shaky voice asked. "Is that you?"

"Who's calling?"

"Cassidy, it's me. Moriah."

Cassidy's heart skipped a beat. "Moriah, what's going on?"

"You were right, Cassidy," Moriah rushed. "This place and the people here aren't what I thought they would be. I want out. Can you help me?"

"Of course. Let me come get you."

"I only have an hour until I'm supposed to get married. But I can meet you in the woods at the south side of the compound. But you have to come now. Otherwise, they'll find me."

Cassidy glanced back at Lisa and frowned. She

could do this. She could help Moriah and still be there for Lisa. "I'll be right there. Just hold tight."

"Hurry, Cassidy. Hurry."

Cassidy ended the call. She hated to go anywhere near Gilead's Cove alone. She'd promised Ty she'd take him with her, but he was out with Braden right now.

She nibbled her bottom lip.

She couldn't pass up this opportunity. Moriah had sounded so scared. She had to help her.

Grabbing her keys, Cassidy started toward her car.

She would go get Moriah, take her somewhere safe, and come back here. No problem.

She hoped.

———

TY AND BRADEN cruised on the water back toward Lantern Beach. Ty had told Braden he would go alone to pick up the rings, but Lisa had insisted that Braden go with him.

The man was so excited to get married he'd been pacing all day, so Lisa probably wanted to keep him occupied for a little while.

"So how are things at Hope House?" Braden asked over the roar of the motor and the splashing of the water on the speedboat Wes had let them borrow.

Ty frowned at the question and pushed his sunglasses up higher.

"They could be better." With a heavy heart, Ty told

him about the possibility of canceling the next session. Braden had been one of the first participants at the retreat center.

"Oh, man," Braden said. "How long do you have until you have to let people know?"

"I need to make some phone calls on Monday." The time was squeezing in. Ty had been hoping for the best, but none of his leads had panned out.

"Wow, I'm sorry to hear that. I know Hope House helped me a lot. I'd hate to see you have to close down after just opening."

"That flood caused more damage than I thought, and even though we had insurance, there was a lot we had to pay out of pocket. I'll probably get reimbursed eventually, but not in enough time."

"I'll pray that the funding comes in," Braden said. "But I've been thinking about something lately."

"What's that?"

"All these guys you're bringing in for the retreat . . . the ex-military," Braden started. "They all are looking for new careers after being out of the military. Have you ever thought about branching out and offering them jobs? Maybe some of the funding could help pay for the retreat center itself."

"You mean recruit from the retreat center?"

"No, I mean maybe branching out and starting a subsidiary? Maybe a company to employ them once they're back on their feet. They would want something a little more high adrenaline than a retreat center. I'm thinking maybe hiring them out as bodyguards or PIs or something."

"It's an interesting thought." Ty had never considered such a service.

"Having the right job can give them a sense of purpose again, you know."

Braden raised a good point—a program like that could pay for the daily operations of Hope House. He'd need to think about that a little more, though. It wasn't a decision that could be taken lightly.

"Speaking of which, are you going to apply with the LBPD for the summer?" Ty asked, turning the attention back to Braden.

"I'm hoping to. My doctor cleared me, but I figured I should wait until after my honeymoon."

"Maybe a good idea."

"Besides, I thought Lisa could use some help getting the restaurant ready for the season. But you really should think about what I said—about starting a company to employ these guys. I could help in the off-season, if you're interested."

"I'll think about it," Ty said. "I agree that people seem to operate through life better when they have a sense of purpose and direction."

Unfortunately, that was Anthony Gilead's whole philosophy also. Only Ty would try to fill that need in a manner that wasn't self-serving.

Ty's phone rang, and he answered without looking to see who was calling.

"Ty?" a female said.

"Yes?" The voice sounded familiar, but he couldn't immediately place it.

"It's Serena."

"Serena?" Ty repeated, uncertain if he'd heard correctly over the roar of the boat's motor.

"Ty, Cassidy needs you. Now."

CHAPTER TWENTY-NINE

CASSIDY PARKED her SUV on the side of the road, out of sight from the main entrance to Gilead's Cove, just as Moriah had asked.

Making sure her gun was in place, she started through the woods to the spot where Moriah had told her to meet.

She'd called both Dane and Leggott to see if either were available to meet her here, but they were both occupied with a domestic dispute at one of the rental houses. Mac was at the town administration office reviewing some election details. And Ty was with Braden, coming back from Hatteras.

Cassidy was going to have to do this alone.

She was just glad that Moriah had finally seen the light, so to speak. If the woman stayed a part of Gilead's Cove, she was just going to be in for a lifetime of hurt and pain. She was thankful Moriah had actually called and asked for help.

She only hoped this rescue operation went off without a hitch.

In some ways, it was better if it was just Cassidy. Too many people might spook the woman or even alert others at Gilead's Cove of what was happening. Cassidy could be quiet and subtle. Besides, Moriah seemed to trust her.

She tromped through the forest, her legs brushing against the thick underbrush.

Cassidy would find Moriah. Take her to her SUV. From there, they would go back to Cassidy's place, she decided. Until she knew if there was a traitor within the police department, she couldn't trust that the woman would be okay if left there.

Yet she couldn't leave her at the cottage by herself either. She figured she would call either Gabe Abbott or Tate Donovan about staying until she could get back. Abbott was a better choice, but she still didn't quite trust the man. Tate was an EMT, but she didn't know the man well.

Either way, Cassidy would make this work. That was certain.

She glanced ahead. It wasn't much farther to their meeting spot—thank goodness. Cassidy had never been a big fan of the woods. Probably because she'd grown up in the city. Either way, something about them spooked her.

At once, the threatening text message she'd gotten this week filled her mind.

I know who you are.

A chill raced up her spine. Who had sent those texts? What was his or her plan for Cassidy? How long would they draw this out before they spilled the truth to anyone who was listening?

She couldn't think about it. Not now. Right now, she'd deal with Moriah. One problem at a time.

She spotted the fence ahead where she was supposed to meet Moriah. The woman wasn't in sight. Not yet, at least. Maybe she was hiding, hoping she wouldn't be caught by any members of Gilead's Cove.

Today wasn't only Lisa and Braden's wedding. No, today was supposed to be Moriah and Gilead's also. If Cassidy could get to the girl before she said, "I do" . . .

Cassidy stepped forward, ready to call out Moriah's name. But, before she could, a hand covered her mouth and a deep voice said, "Thanks so much for coming, Cassidy."

———

"SAY THAT AGAIN, SERENA." Ty tensed as he held the phone to his ear and struggled to hear against the noises around him.

"I think Moriah set Cassidy up," Serena whispered. "You've got to help her. I think she's in danger."

Ty's breath caught. "Where are you, Serena?"

"I'm at the Cove," she rushed. "Moriah and Gilead got married, but I overheard Moriah talking to someone. I sneaked away and found a phone up in an office so I could call you, but I can't get caught. I don't know what they'll do to me if they find out."

The tension in Ty's chest pulled tighter and tighter. "Where do you think Cassidy is, Serena?"

"In the woods outside the compound. You've got to hurry, Ty. These guys Moriah was talking with . . . they looked scary. I don't know what's going on, but I don't like it."

"I'm on my way." He threw the boat into high gear and sped toward the area Serena had mentioned.

"What's going on?" Braden asked, a knot between his eyes.

"Cassidy is in trouble. I've got to go see if I can help her." He glanced at his friend. "I'll get you back in time for your wedding. Don't worry."

"Cassidy first," Braden said. "Let's go."

Ty turned the boat and headed away from the fishing center and toward Gilead's Cove. The compound backed up against the Pamlico Sound. As he got closer, the water became shallower, and he slowed.

When he could go no farther, Ty anchored the boat and jumped into the frigid water. He hurried toward the shoreline near the woods, where Serena had directed him. Water sloshed around him and seaweed grabbed at his legs.

He only hoped the bad guys didn't see him coming.

He needed the element of surprise here if he was going to have the upper hand.

Braden stayed beside him.

Ty's pulse pounded with every step. What if something had happened to Cassidy?

No, he couldn't think like that. In fact, he thought like that all the time. Too often.

The water splashed around him until he reached the sandy shore. Ty wasted no time once he got there. He rushed through the woods, toward the area where Serena said Moriah and Cassidy were supposed to meet.

But when he got there, the area was empty. Only trees and underbrush and marsh grass had invaded the area.

Had Serena been wrong?

"See anything?" Braden paused beside him and drew in deep breaths.

"No, nothing," Ty muttered, an ache forming in his chest.

Just as he said the words, he spotted something on the ground. He reached down and carefully picked it up.

It was Cassidy's gun.

The blood left his face.

This wasn't good.

No, if Cassidy had left her gun behind, then she was in major trouble.

CHAPTER THIRTY

CASSIDY OPENED her eyes and blinked. As an aching pulse pounded at her head, she desperately tried to recall where she was and what had happened.

That's when everything hit her.

She'd gone to meet Moriah. But the woman hadn't been there in the dense woods.

Instead, a hand had gone over her mouth before something hard hit her head.

Everything had gone black.

And now Cassidy was here.

In the woods. Surrounded by trees. The steady song of insects and frogs hung in the air, sounding like a death chant to her now.

Cassidy jerked, trying to move, to get away, to run.

She couldn't. She was . . . tied to a tree. Ropes encircled her, immobilizing her arms against her.

What?

She jerked again, desperate to get away.

It was no use. These ropes were tied tight—so tight she'd probably begin to lose circulation soon.

Keep your wits about you. You can figure this out.

Cassidy surveyed the area around her, trying to find the person or persons who'd done this to her.

And what about Moriah? What had happened to Moriah?

Had those men found her? Had Gilead sent them to retrieve Moriah and make Cassidy pay?

She hoped not. She hoped Moriah was okay. That she hadn't made it to the spot in time. That she'd been spared any of this.

No one was here with her, Cassidy realized. She only saw those trees and the marsh grass and sandy crevices where the forest had invaded the dunes.

But just as she realized that, a shadow appeared from behind her.

She gasped as a man came into view. Flinching, she wanted to raise her arms to fight. But it was no use—she couldn't.

It was . . . James Waldron.

This was the man who'd gone with Reagan to purchase those stuffed animals. Most likely, he was the man who'd killed those people as well—who'd poisoned them. Who'd poisoned Bob. Who'd shot at Cassidy and later put Jimmy James in the hospital after throwing that grenade.

"Well, I see you're okay, Chief Chambers." Waldron

bounced a gun in his hands like it was a toy. "Thanks for coming."

She sneered at him. "You're not Moriah."

"We decided to take her place." He smiled, looking just as mean as Cassidy had imagined him to be.

"Is she okay?" Cassidy asked. "Where is she?"

"She's fine, and that's not important."

"Did you do something to her?" Cassidy couldn't let this go. She needed to know what had happened to the girl.

"We forced her to make that phone call," he said. "I'm sorry we had to do that, but it was the only way to get you out here."

"Why did you want to get me out here?" Cassidy almost didn't want to ask the question. Did she really want to know what they were planning?

Waldron paced in front of her. "So we can finally silence you for once and for all."

"And this was the way you decided to do it?" Cassidy shook her head, trying to plant doubts in the man's mind. It would buy her some time. However, another shadow appeared on the other side of her.

He must be Waldron's sidekick. The man was quiet, obviously the follower of the two. But still, it would be hard for Cassidy to take both of them—if she even had the chance. As it stood right now, there was no way she could get out of these ropes unless someone released her.

These two had no intention of doing that.

"Every time we saw you, there were people around you," Waldron said, still bobbing that gun in his hands. "You weren't exactly an easy target. And then you somehow survived the incident on the boat yesterday, which leads us to this."

Cassidy managed to pull a piece of bark from the tree. Holding it carefully in her hand, she rubbed it against the rope. It was a long shot that this would work, but at least it was something. She just needed to keep him talking.

"Why kill me?" she asked. "There are other people involved here. Why target me?"

"We know you're the one who won't give up." Waldron paused for long enough to shake his head and look halfway impressed at her tenacity.

"So you were selling or smuggling drugs through stuffed animals. You had Reagan and her friends helping you. At some point, you must have gotten scared, so you poisoned them and dumped their bodies. Strange way to kill someone. Why not just shoot them?"

"Because then if their bodies were ever discovered, it would look suspicious. No one was supposed to figure this out."

"But I did."

He scowled. "Exactly. You did it. You messed everything up."

Cassidy couldn't be 100 percent sure, but she didn't think these were the guys who'd sent her those text messages. Nothing they said alluded to that.

Cassidy swallowed hard, anxious to know what they were going to do with her—and to buy time. Maybe someone would find her out here. She'd told Leggott and Dane where she was going, at least.

"What's your plan?" she asked.

Waldron reached behind him and pulled a water bottle from his pocket. Slowly, he twisted the cap until little streams of water spilled over the sides and onto his hands. "I thought it would be poetic if you took a few sips. You know, things would come full circle and all."

Cassidy's blood went cold. Just a few sips, and what would her heart do?

It would stop, just like Bob's had. Just like Reagan's.

And she was helpless to do anything about it.

———

BRADEN LEANED DOWN and touched a broken branch near the ground. "It looks like whoever was here left a trail."

Ty knelt beside him and examined the broken branch. "You're right. It does. Do you think we can follow it?"

"Let's try."

Following Braden's lead, Ty walked through the forest. He wished he could move faster, but he knew tracking didn't work that way. One wrong move, and they'd lose the trail and have to backtrack.

Adrenaline pumped through Ty's veins as reality hit him.

They had Cassidy. Those men—those dangerous men—had the woman he loved.

He could hardly bear the thought of it.

Please, Lord, watch over her. Protect her. She doesn't deserve this.

He squelched the panic that tried to rise in him. Panic would get him nowhere. If there was one thing being a SEAL had taught him, it was that. But when it was the life of someone you loved that was on the line, all bets were off. The training that had been ingrained in him became a distant memory.

"Any idea who these guys are?" Braden asked, kneeling down to examine more foliage.

"We believe they're involved in some drug trade in this area."

"Not affiliated with Gilead's Cove?"

Ty pushed back a prickly branch, ignoring the scrapes on his hand. "If they are, we haven't found the connection. But Gilead is slick. He knows how to cover his tracks. And the fact that Serena called me means there may be some relationship."

Braden grunted. "Gilead has got to be funding his 'organization' somehow."

"People who join pretty much give everything they own to the man." Ty thought it was a shame that people believed so easily, that they were so desperate that they set aside all logic. Then again, Ty supposed some people saw him and his faith in the same way. Though Ty knew it was different, he would have trouble convincing others of that.

"I'd imagine they don't own much," Braden continued. "Most of them seem pretty simple."

Ty bypassed some broken trees, sweat trickling down his back as the day heated up. "That could be true. We can only hope everything comes crashing around him and these people come to their senses."

"You really don't like him, do you?" Braden glanced back at him.

"No, I don't. For several reasons. I don't trust Anthony Gilead at all." Ty stopped and grabbed Braden's arm. He put a finger over his lips and nodded toward the distance.

Voices. He'd heard voices.

Slowly, carefully, Ty and Braden crept forward and stopped behind a tree.

Two men were talking ten feet away.

One of them held a bottle.

Ty slipped behind another tree, desperate to see who these men were addressing.

He sucked in a quick breath when he spotted Cassidy tied to a tree.

He had to get to her and quickly. Because he had a feeling he knew exactly what was inside that bottle.

CHAPTER THIRTY-ONE

"I'M NOT GOING to drink that," Cassidy said through gritted teeth as she stared at the liquid sloshing in the plastic bottle in front of her face.

Waldron laughed in front of her, the sound sardonic and heartless. "Oh, we'll see about that."

She pressed her lips shut and turned her head as he pushed the bottle closer, pressing the round top against her lips until liquid spilled out down her chin.

"Okay, okay, I can see you're not in a hurry." A dry, mocking tone scored Waldron's voice as he stepped back. "That's okay. I've got some time. The important thing is that we get you off this island. Life was much simpler when that other guy was police chief—that's what I've heard, at least. He was as clueless as they come."

Cassidy actually agreed with him on that point. But what would killing her prove?

In the long run, Abbott would find these guys. The authorities knew Waldron's name and were actively searching for him.

Waldron and his friend wouldn't get away with any of this.

Unless maybe this was bigger than these two men in front of her now.

That had to be it, she realized. Waldron must be working for someone else.

He paced away from her, bottle still in hand. When he was a safe enough distance away, Cassidy asked, "Why'd you poison those people? Why not kill them another way? I seriously want to know. It doesn't make sense to me."

Waldron shrugged, like it wasn't a big deal. "When I was in the army, I got bored one night and found the book *White Oleander*. I found it inspiring. I never thought I'd use what I learned . . . until I found that oleander bush in my backyard."

"I guess you started developing a plan after that."

"I did. I knew death by poisoning was more of a chick thing—I figured that would work to my advantage as well. Figuring everything out was actually kind of fun. I knew if I played my cards right, authorities—if they ever found the bodies—might not even realize these people had been murdered."

Cassidy continued to work the ropes, the action becoming more desperate with every stroke. "But you buried your victims here on the island. You didn't think their bodies would ever be found?"

"I figured the water might wash them away or they'd just decay. That the source of their death wouldn't be found. It worked so well I tried it on Bob Anderson also." He offered a smug grin.

"You really thought you were going to get away with it." Seeing the man's dilated pupils, listening to the slight slur of his words, it became obvious to Cassidy that he was high. He'd somehow managed to pass the drug tests to work for the ferry system, but, right now, he was on something. His thought process was messed up.

"I did. And I would have." His gaze narrowed. "If you hadn't come along."

"You don't seem like a killer, James," Cassidy said.

He twirled around and looked at her, surprise lighting his gaze. "My job doesn't pay much. I had to do something."

"So you recruited people to help you with drugs and then killed them?" Cassidy might as well get as much information as she could before they tried to force her to drink that stuff.

"I only killed them when I had to. When they got too nosy. When they threatened to expose me."

"And Barnabas helped you?"

He chuckled, quickly, sharply. "You know about Barnabas? Yeah, Barnabas recruited me. This was his idea. He talked to me on the ferry when he overheard me chatting with someone about financial concerns. He had a solution for me."

"To stuff flakka into stuffed animals and transport those animals to people who want the drugs?" Her stomach turned at the thought of it.

"That's right. It was a pretty good plan. We told people the toys were for charity. Who was going to question that?"

"What if a child got a hold of it?"

"A child isn't going to pull the stuffing from those animals and find those drugs. Besides, that powder is worth a lot of money. The people who buy them don't let them out of their sight."

"And Moby? You set him up, didn't you? And you used Reagan to assist you. That was the only reason she befriended Moby at all—so he could possibly take the fall for all this." Everything was starting to make sense.

Waldron chuckled again. "You're pretty smart. You got further than I thought you would. Yes, I believe in always having a backup plan—or two. That's why I put those anchors around their necks. I figured it would throw police off my tail and buy me some time if the bodies were ever discovered. Meanwhile, Reagan was desperate for another hit and for a means to support herself. She was willing to do whatever was necessary."

"Did you send the pictures to Isaac?"

"We did. That nosy man sees everything. He was always there on his pier, watching us when we went past. If he'd thought about it hard enough, he would have been able to ID us. We slipped those pictures under his door with a letter—he probably didn't tell you about that part."

"What did the letter say?"

"That if he told anyone about us, we'd make sure his sinkers showed up on the police's radar. You know all that man wants is to be left alone."

"And the man at the wedding shower. Was that you?"

"Wedding shower?" Waldron cocked his lip in a sneer. "What wedding shower?"

Cassidy sucked in a breath. If that hadn't been James then it was probably . . . the man who'd sent those texts and planted those cameras.

She licked her lips and pushed forward. "I don't understand how you knew we'd found the bodies that day."

"I monitored the area all the time. The ferry goes by it. When I was on duty, I saw all the uniforms in the area and knew the bodies had been discovered. My shift ended as soon as we unloaded those passengers. I hopped on the boat and knew I needed to try and deter you."

Cassidy nodded. "It was a risky move."

"I'm a risky kind of guy. It's the reason I joined the army." The gleam returned to his gaze.

"And the reason you go around carrying a grenade? Is that because you're a risky kind of guy also?"

"That's right. You never know when you might need

one." He raised the bottle. "Just like you never know when you might need some of this."

He walked closer, the bottle still raised high enough to meet her lips.

Cassidy pressed her lips together again and prepared for the worst. Because her ropes were just as snug as ever.

———

TY SAW the man raise the bottle to Cassidy's lips again. He and Braden had heard everything and knew these were the guys responsible for the recent deaths on the island.

Ty also knew they had to move quickly in order to save the woman he loved.

He motioned for Braden to go to the other side. They'd take these men by surprise.

Just as the man thrust the bottle toward Cassidy's lips and water spilled around her face, Ty lunged from the cover of the forest and tackled the man.

As he did, the other man yelled out.

But Braden was there waiting.

He took the man down and easily pinned him to the ground.

As James Waldron's elbow ribbed Ty, Ty put the man in a headlock. He had nowhere else to go and nothing else to do. After a couple minutes without air,

Waldron's hand hit the ground like a wrestler begging for mercy.

Ty loosened his grip for long enough to grab the man's hands and pull them behind him. He reached into his pocket and pulled out some zip ties. His friends made fun of him, but he never left home without them.

After securing Waldron, he helped Braden subdue the guy's friend.

Then he went to release Cassidy. He pulled out his pocketknife and began working the ropes.

"You had me scared there for a minute," Ty told Cassidy, relieved that she was okay and in one piece. "You didn't drink any of that water, did you?"

"I didn't. It just spilled all over my face. But if you hadn't gotten here in time . . ."

She shuddered. As the ropes fell away from her, she stepped into his arms and rested for a moment in his embrace.

But they didn't have long to stay here.

Cassidy took a step back. "Did you call for backup?"

"Dane is on his way now."

Cassidy turned to Braden. "Go. You have a wedding to get to."

"Are you sure?" Braden asked, glancing at his watch. The ceremony would start in an hour and a half.

"More than sure. Go. We'll be fine."

"Okay." Braden nodded, still looking uncertain. "I'm glad you're okay, Cassidy."

"You won't be okay if you miss your wedding," she told him. "Go!"

Braden took off.

When he was gone, she stepped closer to James Waldron, glowering down above him. "Did Anthony Gilead have anything to do with this?"

"Who?" He spit on the ground, acting like he'd swallowed some sand as he glared up at Cassidy.

"Anthony Gilead."

"Never heard of him." His left eye twitched as he said the words.

"He's running for mayor. Does that ring any bells?"

"Don't know him," James insisted.

"Then how do you know Moriah?"

Waldron scowled. "We found her walking in the woods."

Cassidy shook her head as she glanced down at him. "I find it hard to believe you've never heard Anthony Gilead's name and that you just happened to stumble upon Moriah Roberts."

"I couldn't care less about this island or whoever this guy is you're talking about."

"That's obvious." Cassidy scowled.

Just then, Dane and Leggott showed up.

Cassidy let them take over the investigation.

Cassidy and Ty also had a wedding to get to, and they were going to be pushing it to make it in time.

CHAPTER THIRTY-TWO

CASSIDY SQUEEZED Ty's hand as she watched Lisa and Braden exchange vows before they sealed their marriage with a kiss. They'd chosen to get married on the beach, and the weather had cooperated nicely.

The sun set behind the couple, casting pinks and blues across the sky as Pastor Jack stood before them, presiding over the ceremony. Lisa had decided against having any bridesmaids in favor of something simpler.

It was just beautiful. Beautiful and perfect. Cassidy needed something like this to end her day. To end her week.

Because what a week it had been.

Dane and Leggott were handling the arrests until Cassidy could make it back into the station. She was determined to celebrate her friends first. She would stay at their reception for at least an hour—maybe more.

Then she would continue to fulfill her obligations as police chief.

Gilead's words wouldn't be true in her life. She wouldn't always work to please people and wouldn't find affirmation only in what she offered other people.

But part of that also meant that she had to have a life outside her job. In order to make that happen, she had to set boundaries.

Besides, Abbott was officially in charge of this case. The problem was that Cassidy considered this her island. She felt it was her personal responsibility to ensure everyone was okay.

Cassidy still had a lot of questions that needed to be answered. What exactly was Moriah's role in Cassidy's abduction today? Had she set Cassidy up? Or was it like Waldron had said—had they forced Moriah into cooperating?

Later, she would go talk to Moriah and find out. Cassidy and Ty had paid a quick visit to Gilead's Cove, only to be told that Gilead and Moriah were away on their honeymoon at an undisclosed location.

After they swung by the compound, Cassidy had just enough time to go home and change into something more presentable than the muddy clothes she had on. She'd pulled her hair back into a loose braid, sprayed some perfume, and decided it would have to do.

She was thankful to be alive. Cassidy had been so close to tasting that drug-laced water. To having it go down her throat and enter her system. To having it claim her organs and suck the life from her.

Just as it had with Reagan and Bob. The two other victims would soon have names. Abbott's interrogation of James and his friend should provide the answers.

After the ceremony concluded, everyone headed to the Crazy Chefette to celebrate. The joy on Lisa and Braden's faces nearly made Cassidy forget about everything else that had gone wrong in recent days.

As Cassidy drank some sherbet punch spiked with jalapeno juice, Ty sidled up beside her. "Guess what?"

"What?"

"I just got a call from an old friend who attended the first session at Hope House. John Melton. Do you remember him?"

"How could I forget him?" The man had been a SEAL with Ty. He had more tattoos than anyone Cassidy had ever seen, rode a Harley, but he had a heart of gold.

"John said he appreciated the time he had at Hope House so much that he wanted to do something to say thanks," Ty continued.

"Did he know about your financial struggles?"

"No, he didn't. He said he didn't tell me about this in advance just in case the event was a bust. But he organized a motorcycle rally just for Hope House. Anyway, you'll never believe how much money he raised."

"How much?"

"Fifty thousand dollars."

Cassidy's jaw dropped. "No way."

"Way. Can you believe it?" Ty grinned, looking amazed at how things had worked out.

"It looks like you can buy those plane tickets for this next session after all."

"Yes, I can."

Cassidy threw her arms around him. "That's fantastic, Ty. I'm so happy for you."

"Me too. And I'm glad you're safe. More than glad. I'm forever grateful."

"One of these days, I'll stop putting myself in these situations."

Ty kissed her cheek and stepped back, some of the light leaving his eyes. "Anything more from this guy who's sending the texts?"

She frowned at the reminder. "No, nothing else."

"You don't think it was James Waldron, do you?"

She shook her head. "No, I really don't."

"What about Gilead?"

Cassidy shrugged, still wrestling with the thoughts herself. "I think he's a possibility. But I have nothing to prove it. Then, again, it could be anyone. I have no clues really as to whom this person is. Nor do I have any idea who left those cameras in our cottage or what they plan on doing with any information they may have obtained because of it."

"What about the traitor who's feeding information to Gilead?"

Cassidy squeezed Ty's hand and glanced around the room at each of her friends. Braden and Lisa. Austin and Skye. Wes. Mac. Clemson.

Grief pressed down on her heart. "I just don't know, Ty. I wish I did. I don't want to believe anyone I trust would do this. But I do have to proceed with caution."

"Yes, you do."

Just as Ty said the words, Cassidy's phone buzzed. It was another text message.

You're living on borrowed time.

The blood drained from her face as she showed it to Ty and glanced around again. No one looked her way.

Could the person sending these texts be here at the wedding? Was he watching her now? And what would this mean for her future?

Ty wrapped his arm around her.

Cassidy didn't know. But with Ty by her side, she knew anything was possible—even defeating this unseen enemy and somehow breaking up Gilead's Cove and getting Serena back.

She just needed time. A little more time.

"I'm not leaving, Ty," she muttered.

"What do you mean?"

"I mean, no one is going to scare me away from Lantern Beach." Cassidy raised her head. "I want to grow old here. Watch my friends get married. See their babies. I want to have babies, and I want them to grow up here."

Ty smiled—the action layered with emotion from joy to a touch of sadness. "I like that idea, Cassidy."

"Then let's make it happen. Our saying has been: no one stands alone. Now my mantra is going to be to stand my ground."

"We're all standing it with you, Cassidy. You can count on that."

As the crowd around Lisa and Braden cheered in the background, Cassidy tried to keep the reality of the lingering threat on her life at bay.

She was more than counting on her community here on Lantern Beach to stand with her. Her life depended on it. And so did this island's.

COMING IN APRIL: DEAD ON ARRIVAL

LANTERN BEACH P.D., BOOK 4

By Christy Barritt

CHAPTER 1

Moriah Gilead laced her fingers with her husband's as they walked through a crowd of people, shaking hands and offering words of affirmation. Everyone around them adored this man—and for good reason.

Anthony Gilead was amazing.

The two of them had arrived back from their honeymoon only one day ago. Anthony—who was Moriah kidding? He'd always be Gilead to her—had taken her to a secluded cabin in the mountains of North Carolina. They hadn't left the location all week.

Her cheeks flushed at the thought.

Their walk past the residents of Gilead's Cove ended with Gilead taking the small stage at the front of the room.

Today was the big day. Election day.

Moriah had no idea Gilead was even running for mayor until three days ago.

A lump formed in her throat at the memory.

She thought Gilead should have mentioned that fact to her earlier. But he must have had good reason not to. Moriah had to stop being so quick to judge.

She remained by the wooden steps leading to the stage, at the side of the crowd, and held her hands in front of her like a good, supportive wife. A *submissive* wife. Gilead had many conversations with her about this new role she'd taken on and what it meant.

"Residents of Gilead's Cove and followers of the Cause," Gilead started, gripping the podium as his engaged expression latched onto anyone listening. "It's great to be back with you."

Everyone cheered.

Today's event was a change from the normal morning pep session Gilead led. Something about him getting married, going away, and running for mayor seemed to ignite something in his followers. They were so excited and happy for him.

"Today is going to be a good day," he said, flashing a bright smile.

More cheers.

Gilead obviously felt confident he was going to win this election. And why shouldn't he? The man was smart and charming. He had a way about him that made people want to do things for him. That was a great trait for a leader.

"So, how was your honeymoon?" someone whispered.

Moriah glanced over and saw Ruth had sidled up beside her. The woman had been Moriah's mentor when she'd first arrived here at the Cove. The two of them hadn't spoken since Moriah had returned from her trip, and Moriah had no desire to talk to the woman about anything personal now.

Though it *would* be nice to talk to *someone* about personal things. To whisper secrets and share the highs and lows of her new marriage. Maybe even someone Moriah could ask advice from without fear of being reprimanded.

Instead, Moriah offered a tight smile. "It was wonderful."

Ruth quirked a shaggy eyebrow. "Glad to hear that."

Moriah nibbled on the inside of her cheek. If she were talking to a trusted friend right now, she might tell the truth. Might share that her honeymoon hadn't been anything like she'd imagined.

In her mind, the trip would be full of tender moments where she and Gilead bonded together as husband and wife. After all, they still had so much to learn about each other. Their courtship had been short and hurried, to say the least.

Instead of tender moments, the whole experience had felt like an exercise in . . . greed and insatiability.

Moriah swallowed hard. She would never say those words aloud. Besides, no one would believe her. Everyone thought Gilead was God.

Her expectations for their trip had simply been

unrealistic. Still, she ran a hand over her lips, wishing she could erase the feel of her husband's mouth against hers.

What had once seemed forbidden and romantic now caused nausea to rise in her.

She would adjust. Eventually, she'd tell Gilead her concerns over their relationship. Certainly something between them would change when she did. He'd understand that Moriah needed more of a personal connection and that otherwise she simply felt like a cheap escort.

"Why do you look pale?" Ruth's eyes bore into Moriah.

"I don't look pale," Moriah insisted, hating how her muscles tensed at the question.

"Don't tell me you don't look pale. I'm looking right at you."

Moriah shrugged. "It's a big day. That's all."

"We're all headed into town to vote later. You too?"

"I haven't lived here for long enough, and I didn't know—" She stopped herself before she said too much.

"You didn't know your husband was running for mayor?" Was that delight in Ruth's voice? Was the woman looking for cracks in their marriage so she could exploit them? Or so she could feel better about herself?

The last thing Moriah wanted was anyone feeling sorry for her—or like they had the upper hand.

"We didn't have much time to talk before we got married," Moriah said. "It's not a big deal."

"I'd say it was. If he wins this election, your life is going to look different. He's going to have other responsibilities besides Gilead's Cove. Other priorities besides you."

"I trust my husband, but I'm still not sure why he wants this."

Ruth leaned closer to be heard over Gilead's motivational talk. "Power, my dear. Power."

Just as Ruth said the words, the back doors to the Meeting Place opened. Twenty people Moriah had never seen before flooded inside.

She sucked in a quick, surprised breath. "What . . .?"

"We're busing them in," Ruth whispered. "Isn't it wonderful?"

Moriah's hand clutched the fabric of her dress near her neck. "Busing them in from where?"

"Everywhere. The scouts have begun recruiting. We're expecting to get twenty or thirty more people every week now. We need to expand. But first we need the proper permits."

Realization hit Moriah. Permits? Was that really why Gilead was interesting in taking over Lantern Beach? So he could do what he wanted when he wanted how he wanted?

That sounded like her husband—in more than one way.

She tried to push aside her anxiety, but it wouldn't subside.

Something bad was going to happen here.

Moriah could feel it in her gut. And she had no choice but to trust her husband. Otherwise, she'd face the wrath of the Council, wrath that Gilead had told her included a whip and other punishments she couldn't even imagine suffering.

Cassidy Chambers pulled her oversized sweatshirt closer and melted against her husband as he stepped up behind her. With a cup of coffee in hand and the morning sun shining just above the horizon, the day promised to be a good one.

She could use a good day. In her short tenure as police chief, too many things here on Lantern Beach had gone wrong. Too many crimes. Conspiracies. Threats.

It had accumulated in Cassidy as shoulders that were constantly tight, a body that continually craved caffeine, and a distant headache that frequently wanted to rear.

"Things are going to turn around," Ty murmured in Cassidy's ear, as if sensing her heavy thoughts.

"I know." Cassidy rested her free hand on top of her husband's, treasuring the fact that he was her safe place. Always. "I'll just be happy to have this election over with."

Today the town would elect their new mayor. Three people were in the running: current mayor Mike Tomlinson, former police chief Mac MacArthur, and newcomer Anthony Gilead.

"You don't really think Anthony Gilead is going to win, do you?" Ty seemed to read her thoughts yet again.

Cassidy caught her bottom lip and nibbled on it as she frowned. "I want to say no. I really do. But I've seen crazier things happen before, so I never say never."

"Yeah, I get that."

She drew in a deep breath, trying to wrap her mind around everything that would be transpiring today. Though she'd been a detective in Seattle, this would be her first small-town election. It proved to be more stressful than she ever imagined.

"So there are two voting locations here on the island," Cassidy said, voicing her thoughts aloud. "My crew and I will be busy all day monitoring those sites. We don't anticipate any trouble but . . . we are on Lantern Beach."

"Plus there are town officials who will be monitoring those locations for election fraud. Everything will be okay."

"You think?"

"I do. And tonight, we will be celebrating Mac's win. He's going to make a great mayor."

"He will. He deserves this position. That's for sure." Cassidy stared out at the ocean as it lapped the shore in wave after wave, the motion as certain as the sunrise each morning. The constants in her life were what reassured her—the water, Ty, her circle of friends, God.

Ever since Cassidy had begun receiving some text messages that threatened to reveal her past identity, her peace of mind had scattered. Someone knew who she really was, and that put her—as well as everyone she cared about—in danger.

"That was some party we had for Mac last night." Ty's chin dipped down and rested near her neck.

Cassidy took another sip of her coffee. "I wish I could have made it. I'm still not sure why someone would try to steal a car on an island. As soon as they try to leave on the ferry, they're going to be caught."

"No one ever said criminals were smart."

"I can't argue with that," Cassidy said. "But I heard Lisa really hit it out of the park with her 'Mac-themed' food and drinks."

Mac and cheese with bacon, MacDonald's knockoff Big Macs, MacDaddy sliders and french fries, fried mac-and-cheese balls, and more.

"Doesn't she always go above and beyond?"

"Yes, she does." Their friend Lisa Dillinger had just gotten back from her honeymoon in time to cater and host the event at her restaurant. The turnout had been great.

Cassidy would guess, based on what she'd briefly

seen and heard, that nearly two hundred people had shown up at some point. Considering there were only six hundred locals on the island, Cassidy thought those numbers were outstanding.

Now, Cassidy hoped the turnout at the polls today would reflect all the campaigning that had been done and the qualifications Mac would bring to the office.

Cassidy's phone rang from its position on the railing in front of her.

She sighed and stared at it a moment.

"I knew I should have left it inside." Begrudgingly, she grabbed it and answered. Early morning phone calls were never good. "Chief Chambers."

"Cassidy, it's Doc Clemson. We have a situation I thought you'd want to know about."

"What's going on?"

"We've had about twenty, twenty-five people come in to the clinic this morning with food poisoning."

"Okay . . ." Cassidy wasn't sure what this had to do with her.

"Unfortunately, one of the patients was dead on arrival. I guess the food poisoning when mixed with his already weakened immune system was too much."

"Wow, that's awful. I'm really sorry to hear that."

"Cassidy, there's one thing that everyone here has in common."

She swallowed hard before asking, "What's that?"

"Everyone here was at Lisa's last night."

Cassidy wasted no time getting to the clinic. She wanted to talk to Clemson in person and figure out what was going on here.

But a bad feeling rose in her gut.

This didn't sound good. Not at all.

She bypassed the nurses' station and barely made eye contact with anyone as she walked down the hallway. No, she was a woman on a mission to find answers to protect one of her best friends in the world.

She knocked on Clemson's door before opening it and stepping inside. He looked up from his desk and pushed his glasses higher on his nose. A frown dug into his wrinkled face.

"Thanks for coming, Cassidy. Have a seat."

She sat and stared at the town's only doctor and esteemed medical examiner. "As you can imagine, I'm anxious to hear more. Are you certain it's food poisoning?"

He glanced up and let out a long breath. "Certain? No. Nearly certain? Yes. We'll send samples to the lab, of course. But the fact that everyone who is ill ate at Lisa's last night confirms that this isn't just a virus."

"You said one person died?" The words burned in Cassidy's throat. She hated to even think about it.

"That's correct. Darrell Johnson. He had lupus. His body just couldn't handle everything."

Cassidy shook her head, trying to come to terms

with what she'd learned. Everything about it made her feel sick to her stomach. "I Just can't believe this, Clemson. How is everyone else doing?"

Clemson glanced at the stack of papers in front of him and frowned. "Well, ten more people have been admitted since I called you. Fever. Headache. Chills. Vomiting. It's not a pretty scene out there, and we're running out of room. We may have to call in backup to help because we're not staffed to handle this many sick people."

"But I know Lisa. She's too responsible to let something like this happen."

He lowered the papers, but his frown still remained. He looked tired, like he'd been up all night. He probably had. "It can happen even to the best. Maybe it wasn't Lisa at all. Maybe it was one of the foods she purchased. Maybe there needs to be a recall on some produce or seafood."

"Does everyone else seem okay? No one else is on death's door or anything?" Cassidy prayed that wasn't the case, that this outbreak would subside instead of worsening.

"Not that I know of. Let's hope not."

"What's the next step?" She was the police chief and needed to think like a cop instead of a friend right now. But what was the protocol for something like this? She had no experience in dealing with massive food-poisoning outbreaks.

"I'll have to call the Department of Health. They'll

do an investigation. We need to find the source of this before other people become ill."

That made sense.

Cassidy shifted, knowing that the events about to be set in motion would turn her friend's life upside down. She cleared her throat before asking, "Clemson, have you told Lisa yet?"

He shook his head, the action heavy and burdened. Almost everyone in Lantern Beach loved Lisa and only wanted the best for her. "No, I haven't been able to bring myself to do it."

Cassidy stood. "I will."

She didn't want to do it. Didn't want to see the joy slip from her friend's eyes. She'd looked so happy earlier since returning from her honeymoon. She'd delighted in hosting Mac's party.

And now this.

"You sure?" Clemson asked.

Cassidy nodded. "Yeah, I'm sure. It needs to come from a friend. Plus, I'm going to have to get involved. Someone died. This is much bigger than mere food poisoning at this point. This will shut her restaurant down. It could even lead to some civil cases. It's hard to say right now. But it will probably get uglier before it gets better."

"I'll be praying for everyone involved."

Cassy stood and nodded. "Thank you. This town is going to need it."

ALSO BY CHRISTY BARRITT:

Hidden Currents

You can take the detective out of the investigation, but you can't take the investigator out of the detective. A notorious gang puts a bounty on Detective Cady Matthews's head after she takes down their leader, leaving her no choice but to hide until she can testify at trial. But her temporary home across the country on a remote North Carolina island isn't as peaceful as she initially thinks. Living under the new identity of Cassidy Livingston, she struggles to keep her investigative skills tucked away, especially after a body washes ashore. When local police bungle the murder investigation, she can't resist stepping in. But Cassidy is supposed to be keeping a low profile. One wrong move could lead to both her discovery and her demise. Can she bring justice to the island . . . or will the hidden currents surrounding her pull her under for good?

Flood Watch

The tide is high, and so is the danger on Lantern Beach. Still in hiding after infiltrating a dangerous gang, Cassidy Livingston just has to make it a few more months before she can testify at trial and resume her old life. But trouble keeps finding her, and Cassidy is pulled into a local investigation after a man mysteriously disappears from the island she now calls home. A recurring nightmare from her time undercover only muddies things, as does a visit from the parents of her handsome ex-Navy SEAL neighbor. When a friend's life is threatened, Cassidy must make choices that put her on the verge of blowing her cover. With a flood watch on her emotions and her life in a tangle, will Cassidy find the truth? Or will her past finally drown her?

Storm Surge

A storm is brewing hundreds of miles away, but its effects are devastating even from afar. Laid-back, loose, and light: that's Cassidy Livingston's new motto. But when a makeshift boat with a bloody cloth inside washes ashore near her oceanfront home, her detective instincts shift into gear . . . again. Seeking clues isn't the only thing on her mind—romance is heating up with next-door neighbor and former Navy SEAL Ty Chambers as well. Her heart wants the love and stability she's longed for her entire life. But her hidden identity only leads to a tidal wave of turbulence. As more answers emerge about the boat, the danger around her rises, creating a treacherous swell that threatens to reveal her past. Can Cassidy mind her own business, or will the storm surge of violence and corruption that has washed ashore on Lantern Beach leave her life in wreckage?

Dangerous Waters

Danger lurks on the horizon, leaving only two choices: find shelter or flee. Cassidy Livingston's new identity has begun to feel as comfortable as her favorite sweater. She's been tucked away on Lantern Beach for weeks, waiting to testify against a deadly gang, and is settling in to a new life she wants to last forever. When she thinks she spots someone malevolent from her past, panic swells inside her. If an enemy has found her, Cassidy won't be the only one who's a target. Everyone she's come to love will also be at risk. Dangerous waters threaten to pull her into an overpowering chasm she may never escape. Can Cassidy survive what lies ahead? Or has the tide fatally turned against her?

Perilous Riptide

Just when the current seems safer, an unseen danger emerges and threatens to destroy everything. When Cassidy Livingston finds a journal hidden deep in the recesses of her ice cream truck, her curiosity kicks into high gear. Islanders suspect that Elsa, the journal's owner, didn't die accidentally. Her final entry indicates their suspicions might be correct and that what Elsa observed on her final night may have led to her demise.

Against the advice of Ty Chambers, her former Navy SEAL boyfriend, Cassidy taps into her detective skills and hunts for answers. But her search only leads to a skeletal body and trouble for both of them. As helplessness threatens to drown her, Cassidy is desperate to turn back time. Can Cassidy find what she needs to navigate the perilous situation? Or will the riptide surrounding her threaten everyone and everything Cassidy loves?

Deadly Undertow

The current's fatal pull is powerful, but so is one detective's will to live. When someone from Cassidy Livingston's past shows up on Lantern Beach and warns her of impending peril, opposing currents collide, threatening to drag her under. Running would be easy. But leaving would break her heart. Cassidy must decipher between the truth and lies, between reality and deception. Even more importantly, she must decide whom to trust and whom to fear. Her life depends on it. As danger rises and answers surface, everything Cassidy thought she knew is tested. In order to survive, Cassidy must take drastic measures and end the battle against the ruthless gang DH-7 once and for all. But if her final mission fails, the consequences will be as deadly as the raging undertow.

Lantern Beach Romantic Suspense

Tides of Deception

Change has come to Lantern Beach: a new police chief, a new season, and . . . a new romance? Austin Brooks has loved Skye Lavinia from the moment they met, but the walls she keeps around her seem impenetrable. Skye knows Austin is the best thing to ever happen to her. Yet she also knows that if he learns the truth about her past, he'd be a fool not to run. A chance encounter brings secrets bubbling to the surface, and danger soon follows. Are the life-threatening events plaguing them really accidents . . . or is someone trying to send a deadly message? With the tides on Lantern Beach come deception and lies. One question remains—who will be swept away as the water shifts? And will it bring the end for Austin and Skye, or merely the beginning?

Shadow of Intrigue

For her entire life, Lisa Garth has felt like a supporting character in the drama of life. The designation never bothered her—until now. Lantern Beach, where she's settled and runs a popular restaurant, has boarded up for the season. The slower pace leaves her with too much time alone. Braden Dillinger came to Lantern Beach to try to heal. The former Special Forces officer returned from battle with invisible scars and diminished hope. But his recovery is hampered by the fact that an unknown enemy is trying to kill him. From the moment Lisa and Braden meet, danger ignites around them, and both are drawn into a web of intrigue that turns their lives upside down. As shadows creep in, will Lisa and Braden be able to shine a light on the peril around them? Or will the encroaching darkness turn their worst nightmares into reality?

Lantern Beach P.D.

On the Lookout

When Cassidy Chambers accepted the job as police chief on Lantern Beach, she knew the island had its secrets. But a suspicious death with potentially far-reaching implications will test all her skills—and threaten to reveal her true identity.

Cassidy enlists the help of her husband, former Navy SEAL Ty Chambers. As they dig for answers, both uncover parts of their pasts that are best left buried. Not everything is as it seems, and they must figure out if their John Doe is connected to the secretive group that has moved onto the island.

As facts materialize, danger on the island grows. Can Cassidy and Ty discover the truth about the shadowy crimes in their cozy community? Or has darkness permanently invaded their beloved Lantern Beach?

Attempt to Locate

A fun girls' night out turns into a nightmare when

armed robbers barge into the store where Cassidy and her friends are shopping. As the situation escalates and the men escape, a massive manhunt launches on Lantern Beach to apprehend the dangerous trio. In the midst of the chaos, a potential foe asks for Cassidy's help. He needs to find his sister who fled from the secretive Gilead's Cove community on the island. But the more Cassidy learns about the seemingly untouchable group, the more her unease grows. The pressure to solve both cases continues to mount. But as the gravity of the situation rises, so does the danger. Cassidy is determined to protect the island and break up the cult . . . but doing so might cost her everything.

#9 Broom & Gloom

#10 Dust and Obey

#11 Thrill Squeaker

#11.5 Swept Away (novella)

#12 Cunning Attractions

#13 Cold Case: Clean Getaway

#14 Cold Case: Clean Sweep

While You Were Sweeping, A Riley Thomas Spinoff

HOLLY ANNA PALADIN MYSTERIES:

When Holly Anna Paladin is given a year to live, she embraces her final days doing what she loves most—random acts of kindness. But when one of her extreme good deeds goes horribly wrong, implicating Holly in a string of murders, Holly is suddenly in a different kind of fight for her life. She knows one thing for sure: she only has a short amount of time to make a difference. And if helping the people she cares about puts her in danger, it's a risk worth taking.

THE WORST DETECTIVE EVER:

I'm not really a private detective. I just play one on TV.

Joey Darling, better known to the world as Raven Remington, detective extraordinaire, is trying to separate herself from her invincible alter ego. She played the spunky character for five years on the hit TV show *Relentless*, which catapulted her to fame and into the role of Hollywood's sweetheart. When her marriage falls apart, her finances dwindle to nothing, and her father disappears, Joey finds herself on the Outer Banks of North Carolina, trying to piece together her life away from the limelight. But as people continually mistake her for the character she played on TV, she's tasked with solving real life crimes . . . even though she's terrible at it.

<u>#1 Ready to Fumble</u>

ABOUT THE AUTHOR

USA Today has called Christy Barritt's books "scary, funny, passionate, and quirky."

Christy writes both mystery and romantic suspense novels that are clean with underlying messages of faith. Her books have won the Daphne du Maurier Award for Excellence in Suspense and Mystery, have been twice nominated for the Romantic Times Reviewers' Choice Award, and have finaled for both a Carol Award and Foreword Magazine's Book of the Year.

She is married to her Prince Charming, a man who thinks she's hilarious—but only when she's not trying to be. Christy is a self-proclaimed klutz, an avid music lover who's known for spontaneously bursting into song, and a road trip aficionado.

When she's not working or spending time with her family, she enjoys singing, playing the guitar, and exploring small, unsuspecting towns where people have no idea how accident-prone she is.

Find Christy online at:

www.christybarritt.com

www.facebook.com/christybarritt

www.twitter.com/cbarritt

Sign up for Christy's newsletter to get information on all of her latest releases here: **www.christybarritt.com/ newsletter-sign-up/**

If you enjoyed this book, please consider leaving a review.